THE GIRL

WHO SAW IT ALL

THE GIRL WHO SAW IT ALL

ROOPRASHI

Invincible Publishers

Published by
Invincible Publishers
201A, SAS Tower, Sector 38, Gurugram – 122003
Phone: +91-124-4034247, +91 9355675555
www.i-publish.in

First Published in 2017
Revised Edition in 2020

ISBN: 978-93-89600-75-9

Lipi Gupta
Freelance Editor, Writer, Blogger
(Gully Writers) and Psychologist.

To the unconditional love of my parents....

Praise for the author and her works

"The Ascent Of Love is a story encrypted with motivation and intellect that is highly gripping yet heart-touching. It is recommended to everyone to have a positive outlook in life."

- Radhakrishnan Pillai, Author of 8 Bestsellers

"Jeevan Ko Prerit Karti Hai Pustak The Girl Who Saw It All"

- Dainik Jagran

"Amazon Par Dhoom Macha Rahi Hai Pustak The Girl Who Saw It All"

- Khabar Today

"Rooprashi weaves a strong story through her debut novel."

- Ms. Kena Shree, Writer & Storyteller.

"A genuine book with a gripping story."

- Dr. Subodh Kumar Singh, Kashi Ratna & Peat Prize Awardee.

"A must read. The book doesn't give you 'yes' or 'no' answers to questions; but it instead helps us understand the nature of the questions better, so we can answer them for ourselves."

- Lucknow Book Club

"Author Rooprashi has fantastic narration skills and chosen an important topic. This book can be life changing and will make anyone think about the way we live these days."

- The Daily Brunch Team

"Yuvaon ko prerit karti hai pustak The Girl Who Saw It All"

- Nav Express.

A Note On The Author

Management Executive, author and blogger, **Rooprashi** is an individual brimming with stories. The author whose debut novel "The Girl Who Saw It All" has made waves across the country possesses both compassion and composure and a capacity for empathy that is clearly reflected in her writing. She writes with an aim to motivate her readers and infuse positivity in society.

She has an artistic bent of mind since childhood and was involved in many activities in her school and college. Since, the age of ten, she has been doing stage performances in singing and plays musical instruments like harmonium, piano, and flute. She is also quite active in sports like Table Tennis and has participated in "Artificial Wall Climbing" at National Level.

She loves writing motivational and spiritual pieces as well as quotes. For more info on her writing and updates on her latest articles and books, you can visit her website **www.rooprashi.in**

You can also connect with her:

Facebook- **Rooprashi**

Instagram- **@rooprashi**

CHAPTER 1

"When are you going to take bath today?" Amita grinned waking me up from deep slumber.

"Aarohi, Wake up. We will get late for the class. Wake uppp." She said sweeping the quilt off my face.

"Tell your roommate to take bath first. She is the one you have to stay with." I said lazily covering my face with the quilt again. Though Amita was very well aware that I hated to stand in queue to collect hot water outside the hostel bathroom, still she tried her luck every time to wake me up early. It was an established regime during chilling winters in Chandigarh. But I am a free soul and also clever enough to shift my bath routine to evenings when bathrooms were mostly empty and I can easily enjoy my baths without hassle.

"I am not going to stand in that queue and waste time waiting for my turn when I could catch up with my beauty sleep for an extra hour." I announced from inside the quilt to make sure that Amita had given up on her efforts to wake me up and had left the room. When she did not retort, I assumed that she had gone.

I am pursuing post-graduation in sciences and Amita is my abutting neighbour and friend in hostel. Though I have not been allotted any roommate and am living alone in my room but Amita made sure that I should not have a single lone and tranquil moment in the hostel. In a way, Amita is my family away from family in the hostel. Some people are just those souls that connect and form a bond. Amita is one such friend.

Friends and family play a great role in our life. Our behavior from our childhood itself is determined by the kind of atmosphere we grow in, the personalities around us sway us to the extent we cannot even ideate. Our childhood experiences have an ever-lasting impact on our personalities and get imbibed so well in our sub-conscious minds that they become indivisible part of it. We behave similarly when we face same situations ourselves and it seems so natural to us.

The kids who grow up in a peaceful environment are generally composed while those who grow up watching quarrels in the family are moody and may have anger-issues. Lucky are the kids who have an understanding family and supportive friends. My life is highly influenced by my mother. I always wanted to be like her, self-assured and staunch. There was a time in my life when I was not performing well academically. Nothing seemed to be in control and I was continuously struggling. Though I had passed my tenth class examinations on honor roll, the big question looming in front of me was 'Whether I should opt for Mathematics or Biology?' The kids who get a good percentage are expected to opt for science subjects by default without considering their interests and inclinations.

Engineering and Medical are both considered the major fields, best for a dignified survival. I took up both, biology as I thought I was brilliant enough to do that and Maths because it is considered as an all-life subject. But after a period of four months, I was struggling with my academics. Specially, Physics was giving me a major psychological trauma.

My confidence level had drooped very low. Once among the toppers, I went down to being an average student. This made me silent in class. During those times, it was my mother who supported me, showed confidence in me. When I lost all my hopes, and started believing that I was just a part of the crowd and there was nothing special in me, it was my mother's confidence that did not let me give up and finally I got through the competitive exam for further studies in Punjab University.

This was a life changing moment for me. I was no longer just a regular part of crowd in my mind; I was no longer conscious about myself. I gained my confidence as I was now special in my own eyes. The confidence I once lost was not just revived, but boosted to another level.

When you have a family that uplifts you, you get the strength to face life. This strength not comes just from your family, but you exude it too. Every living species has a family to stick on to. *Birds can glide away easily. But they choose to fly together and never abandon their loved ones.*

"Are you going to skip your breakfast?" Amita's voice rang in my ears again. I was wrong in underestimating her dedication towards disturbing my sleep. She was still there in the room.

"Get ready fast yaar, else we would get late for the class." She said irritated, shaking me as the bed too shook with me.

"Okay... fine. Hunh... I will also sleep with you." She was now pushing me towards the wall to make room for her to sleep on my single bed. She very well knew how much 'Touch Me Not' kind of a person I was. I never understood why friends have to hug each other and pull each other's cheeks. I am a 'Talk from a distance' kind of a person.

I peeped out of the quilt, gave her an irked look and a side glance at the table clock. "Oh My God. We are really getting late. I have to attend that early morning lecture today. My attendance is already short in that one." I said waking up hastily.

"In which language was I trying to tell you this till now? French?" Amita said sarcastically.

"Yeah... yeah. I will be ready in 5 minutes. We won't be late." I said leaving for the bathroom with my towel and toothbrush in hand.

"Be fast. It's Wednesday...." Amita voice echoed in the hostel corridor. It was Wednesday and "Gobhi Ka Parantha" was the breakfast menu which I could not afford to miss. It is my favorite breakfast of the week.

We both were at the breakfast table laden with paranthas, curd and butter in front of us.

"We hog a lot, Aarohi. When are we starting a diet?"

"From tomorrow." I replied, engrossed eating my parantha. I love food (and it was nothing less than Gobhi Ka Parantha) and didn't like to get disturbed with thoughts of dieting while eating my favorite one. It kills the fun of eating.

"Look at Subhan Allah. See, how she is munching brekky like a goat and still has such a handsome and rich boyfriend." Amita said looking at our another neighbor, Rachita who was also having her breakfast at the mess table. She had nicknamed her as 'Subhan Allah' as Rachita was always full of self-praises.

"You know she was flaunting her diamond ring yesterday that her boyfriend gifted her." Amita added.

"She is nice, yaar. Why are you always jealous of her?" I asked sarcastically.

"Nice? from which angle?" Amita said persuading me to look at her again. I started laughing as I looked at her and imagined her to be a goat.

"You have to see her boyfriend. I saw him last Sunday when he came to pick her up from hostel. He is so handsome, yaar." Amita said taking a deep sigh.

"Don't worry you will find a better one. Finish your breakfast fast now. We have to reach the department on time." I said taking the last bite of my parantha.

The phone screen flashed. It was Rudra. I picked up the call. "Good Morning," he said.

I could sense the chirpiness in his voice. "Good Morning. You sound happy."

"Yes, because I am happy. I just got the news of my promotion and the first person I wanted to share it with was you" Rudra sounded excited.

"Wow that is such great news. Congratulations." A smile flashed across my face too.

"And you know what? My salary has also hiked with this promotion. I think now you would run after me requesting to marry you. But who knows my plans might have changed." teased Rudra.

I laughed. I loved the way he teased me with his silly jokes. There was something about him and his simplicity that I felt so attached to. But for me, this was an amazing friendship. I did sometimes wonder, why he made my heart race, but that may be normal for my age.

"Okay, listen. I have to give this good news at my home. I will call you later." Rudra said disconnecting the call.

My day had kick started on such a good note. First 'Gobhi Ka Parantha' and now news of Rudra's promotion. What more could I expect out of a good day.

"What happened? Why are you blushing silently?" Amita asked. We were on our way to our Departments to attend the classes.

"Rudra got promotion in his office and increment in salary." I happily informed.

"That is good news. But why are you so happy? You are blushing like your boyfriend got a raise." Amita said trying to dig into me again.

"No silly. Nothing like that." I laughed and dismissed all her false hopes.

"He loves you, Aarohi. You also always lit up seeing him or even his call. But you always consider your fondness for him as just good friendship. He seems to be a nice guy, yaar, and has given many hints of his love for you. I am sure that sub-consciously you also know that he loves you. Just try to be sure of your feelings for him, yaar." She said looking at me as if she was trying to read my expressions.

"You know na... yaar, I have never been in a relationship earlier and do not know how the concept of love actually fits for me. Having a boyfriend, always, felt like a stupidity to me, but I also know that it is different with Rudra. He feels really special to me. It is just that I can't match him to the concept of love yet. I think I need some more time to be clear in thoughts." I replied.

We had reached Amita's Department. "Okay, fine. I think you are right. We should never be in hurry when it comes to relationships." She said bidding a good-bye as she turned towards her class.

"Bye. See you in the evening" I said waving back to her.

I had few friends since childhood. I never liked to be part of huge groups. I liked my own space and shared my personal life with few selected ones. Amita knew me very well. She knew how sensitive and emotional person I was, while I displayed to be so practical and non-sentimental outside.

CHAPTER 2

My phone was flashing continuously while in the class. Rudra was calling me. I left my class in the middle and went outside to attend the call.

"Hello, what happened?" I said picking up the call.

"Aarohi, I need to talk to you." Rudra said. He sounded tense.

"My parents have been pressurizing me to get married. I am already twenty six, have a decent job and now I have got promotion too. They told me to tell them if I like someone or else they would get me married to the girl of their choice." He said as I listened to him silently.

"I love you, Aarohi and want to get married to you. But you need to take a decision now whether you love me or not. I need to know if you would marry me so that I can tell my parents about you."

"I do not know what to say. I need some time. I will call you in the evening." I told him.

I was sure marriage is not a priority for me at this point of time. I am just twenty. I have not thought about getting into a relationship or getting married. But for him it is. I love the way my life is, the way my relationship with Rudra is. I want nothing more at that point of time. But what if he gets married to someone else? Will I be fine with it? It should not bother me if I consider him just a buddy. I was going through a number of emotional thoughts. As the Bio-chemistry teacher taught about the formation of gene variants and the reactions that take place in the chromosomes, I felt as if all these reactions were going on inside my brain nerves at the moment.

Back in the hostel in the evening, I was pondering over what to tell Rudra about the marriage proposal when he himself called up.

"Have you thought about my proposal, Aarohi?" he asked. It seemed that he had been waiting for this evening eagerly and wanted to know how I felt about him as early as possible.

"Rudra, you are my good friend, and I love you as a friend. You are very dear to me as my best buddy, but I do not love you in any other way. I am not in love with you. I am sorry."

"Are you sure of your decision Aarohi?" he asked sadly. He seemed heart-broken.

"Yes, Rudra," I replied meekly.

"You do not mind if I get married to someone else?" Rudra asked twisting the question.

"No, I do not. You can get married wherever you feel like." I replied in a slow tone.

"That is out of the question now, isn't it?" Catching hold of himself he said "Okay, then I need to stop talking to you. I love you a lot and cannot be just friends with you. I will try to move on in my life and marry the girl of my parent's choice. But I do not want to be in touch with you anymore." There was sadness and anger in Rudra's voice.

I too got emotional hearing this but I had no choice but to agree to him. "Okay. As you wish." I said and disconnected the call.

I knew Rudra was very close to my heart. I was bonded to him with love. I thought that the bond is strong enough to tolerate the ups and downs and things will clear up with time.

I was not in touch with Rudra anymore. Though I visited his social media profiles sometimes but there were no major updates regarding his life. The initial days were fine. But as days passed, I started missing Rudra, his talks, his jokes, the way he made me feel so special.

"These news channels have more funny news than any comedy show." Amita said flipping the TV channels. We were watching TV in the hostel's "Common room" late at night.

"Amita, there is nothing interesting coming on TV. I am going to sleep now. It's already one in night." I said getting up from the sofa.

"Wait. I am also coming with you. I am also sleepy." Amita said switching the TV off with the remote.

"The corridor seems so horrifying at night. So silent and cold." Amita said mischievously as we walked towards our rooms.

"What is going on in your mind?" I asked her, trying to read her face expressions.

"Just wait and watch." She said as she walked towards Subhan Allah's room and knocked her door loudly.

"Run..." she said as she held my hand and we both ran towards Amita's room and hastily entered it.

"What is this noise? What are you doing?" Amita's roommate got up from sleep and asked in husky voice. We could see her outline peeping out of the quilt as it was dark in the room.

"Nothing. Nothing. You sleep." Amita replied her.

"What is going on?" I whispered to Amita.

"I had told Subhan Allah that there is a ghost in the hostel who knocks the doors at night." She whispered back controlling her laugh.

"You are too much. What if she is too scared after this?"

Amita's behavior seemed quite puerile to me.

"At the most she will call her boyfriend and tell him that the ghost in the hostel is also mad for her. Whatever it is, we will come to know in the morning, naa." Amita was still laughing.

"You are evil sometimes. I mean mostly." I laughed lightly.

"I know you are such a divine person and I am a devil. Go to your room and sleep." Amita said.

"Haha. Okay. Good night." I said as I left to go to my room to sleep.

"Should I tell this incident to Rudra?" I had that gut feel again. I felt like calling Rudra every now and then. It was very unusual for me not to share my day and small or big incidents with him.

I had started missing Rudra terribly now. Many times, I would pick up my phone to call him but then I was reminded of his words and thought I would become a hurdle in his life by calling him and reminding him of me.

As the days passed, I was becoming a lifeless person. Rudra seemed to be the charm of my life which I had not realized earlier. I mostly kept silent these days. My life suddenly started feeling very lonely to me. I wouldn't laugh at Amita's or anyone's jokes anymore and kept myself piled up with work. I changed my routine so I don't have to face many people around in corridor.

Amita was worried seeing my condition.

"Why isn't he calling me, Amita? Doesn't he miss me the way I miss him?" I asked her teary eyed.

"Aarohi, you should go home for some days. You need a change. You need to be around your family. It will help you face this." Amita said.

"No yaar. I am fine."

"No, you are not fine, Aarohi. All my efforts to keep you happy are not bearing fruits too. You need your mother, your family around you. Please understand. I am calling Aunty to take you home." She sternly said looking into my eyes.

She called my mother and told her to take me home. I went home after that.

LOVE

Love is an emotion which makes our life worth living. It makes us feel lively. No wonder why the most important organ "HEART" has been associated with love. Love makes our heart beat. Love also makes the heart skip a beat. Love has equal importance in our life as the heart has in our body.

It's commonly said that you fall in love but actually love never makes you fall. Life is meant to fly not sink. With the right person, you never fall in love, you rise. Love helps in every aspect to triumph against the odds. Love conquers everything but only when the feeling is pure and strong.

Sometimes we feel an instant connection with a person while sometimes we don't feel the same even after years of being together. We may develop liking for different people in different phases of life but finding the person with whom our soul connects is rare. They may be miles apart, but are closer to heart. They may be with us or out of sight, but they are always on our mind. We feel their vibes like our own. We feel it every minute with the one we love.

CHAPTER 3

"Do you really want to get married?" my mother asked, surprised.

"Please don't give this surprised look, mom." I said a bit embarrassed. I had never discussed marriage with mom so seriously. It had always been discussed between us in a joking manner.

"No. I mean you were the girl who used to get annoyed on even hearing the word 'marriage'. You always said you'd stay only with us no matter what. I am not saying that's what I want. But are you sure this is what you want at this age?" Mom said reminding me of my own thoughts and I had no answer to this.

I was confused myself. I had fallen in love but had no idea what my next step should be. I am very young and want to study further and have a flourishing career of my choice just like every other student of my age. But Rudra was elder to me and was well settled in his career. His family now wanted him to get married and was bringing up marriage proposals to him every other day. The situation was now becoming difficult for him to handle and he wanted to get married to me as soon as possible.

Seeing my state of mind, mom came to my rescue "Aarohi beta, we come across situations in life where we do not understand what to do. We seek others' advice which at times helps us. But the best advice that we can get comes from our inner-selves. The way we know ourselves, no one else does. Let me tell you a short story. It might help you clear your mind, and take a decision."

"What is the purpose of your life? An entrepreneur asked a saint. He answered "Happiness". "That is not a purpose" the entrepreneur laughed. The saint smiled and asked him "What is the purpose of your life?" The entrepreneur replied "I want to be the best in IT industry. I am expanding my company across the world." "Why do you want to do this?", the saint asked again. "Because I want to earn a lot of money and fame." he replied.

The saint again asked "Why do you want money and fame?" The entrepreneur answered, "To live a luxurious life as I have always dreamed of." The saint smiled and asked "Why do you want to fulfill your dreams?" The entrepreneur replied, irritated this time "Because it gives me happiness." Saint said with a broad smile "That's what I said; the purpose of everyone's life is happiness. It's just that we try to find it in different things."

"Aarohi, you need to decide which situation and happiness you can compromise with. What is important for you in life and what your heart wants to do? Just keep doing what makes your heart happy, everything else will eventually flow in as you walk the path of your life." Mom said.

"Life is a risk and you have to take it as it comes. But do not compromise on what you want to do in your career if you don't want to compromise on it. Remember kid, your happiness is your responsibility. Do not depend on anyone else for that." She added.

"Yes, mom. I will do it. I love him, mom. I think I want to marry him. I want to be with him. I will not stop my work and do everything I want, but after marrying him. Thank you, mom."

"Aarohi, if you have decided this; I will be with you. I'll help you with it if this makes you happy. But you do think over it kid."

I hugged her lovingly. It was such a relief to see her understand my situation. Her advice enabled me to see things clearly. Happy, I was thinking that the world lacks happiness. Though there were enough reasons to smile and be happy. But the negative things attract a human mind more, the negative incidents happening everywhere, sometimes big or small, our bustling schedules, fraught lives and lacking faith contribute to lower number of smiling faces. A single negative thought or incident is enough to spoil our day.

I always wondered at how much the world has become materialistic. Gadgets, clothes and other stuff have taken more important front seat and the most important things like feelings, emotions and beauty in simplicity have been dumped further back. We have even learnt to quantify happiness. Smiling has also become a part of job to keep the customers happy. I used to be amazed to see the salesmen, air staff, shopkeepers smiling whole day and attending their customers and always tried to read their eyes. The person, continuously smiling, may be having the worst day of his life. But he smiles because that is part of his/her job. How frustrating it is to not be able to show true emotions?

I wondered what would make me happy at this point in life. *The hardest of the fights are those we fight within ourselves and that too when we need to choose within two options that are equally significant to us.* We stand opposite in both sides of court. Life sometimes sets the toughest question papers for us. But every question certainly has an answer. The answer may not be clear now, but the mist clears itself with time.

The only answer in my mind was Rudra. I had decided to choose Rudra over everything else I desired and leave rest to destiny. I loved Rudra deeply and had realized it the hard way. It had been four months since we last talked. I decided to call him and tell him how much I loved him. Although I had deleted his number from my phone but his number was deeply imprinted in my mind which I was unable to forget.

THE OTHER ME

It has been rightly quoted by someone "The hardest prison to escape is in your mind". There are two "Me" within me. The one which I appear to be and the other one which is mostly ignored. The one I don't want to accept, the one I know exists but still doesn't, the one I try to overpower, the one who is still a child, the one who is sometimes very mature and the one who is always free. Yes, it is me, the other me.

We live in the world where we have costly watches but no time, big houses but small families, high quality medicines but poor health, lots of friends on social media but no real friend in reality.

We are so much involved in our everyday busy routines and fast life that we have got habitual to ignore the real us and it seems quite normal to us mostly. It seems like a race where everyone is trying to become superhuman with loads of work and responsibilities.

Sometimes we just need to press the pause button and enjoy the moment. Everyone is born as a unique individual. But as we grow up we add up so many layers to ourselves in the race of becoming perfect for the world. During this race we ignore the one person- the real me.

What is there to be proud of even if we win this race? What is so good if you are ignoring yourself and being perfect for the world? Whom we try to impress by being superhuman?

We are mostly too hard on ourselves. Let's not be too harsh with ourselves, let's not be strong always... let's not be perfect. Let's give ourselves a chance to live, to err, to be weak, to breathe, to cry, to laugh, to dance and to express every emotion as it is. We are humans. The essence of life is felt by living the moments and evolving as a human being.

CHAPTER 4

With a thought to surprise Rudra, I called him from a payphone. Rudra picked the call.

"Hello, Rudra. This is Aarohi here."

Rudra was working in his office and so were many others. Lot of background noise was coming from the receiver.

"Hold on, Aarohi." He said happily. He must have come out to talk as the voices died in the background. "How are you, Aarohi?" he asked emotionally.

"I am fine. How are you, Rudra?"

"I am fine too, Aarohi".

"Rudra I really missed you all these days. Separating from you made me realize how important you are to me. You were always right that this bond that we share is love. I love you, Rudra and I want to marry you." I said everything fervently in one go. I did not want to waste any further time and be with Rudra as soon as possible. "I have realized this well that I can only be happy with you or none at all. You have become necessity for my happiness. I am so sorry for being so late..."

"Wait, Aarohi. Please listen to me. I love you too, Aarohi. I love you so very much." Rudra said as if urgently stopping me from saying more; and then suddenly paused. "Aarohi, I need to tell you something."

"Tell me what is it?" I felt curious. I could feel the tension in his voice.

"Aarohi, the day you said no to me, I was very heart broken and angry. I wept that day. I got a call from my parents and they asked me about my answer to a marriage proposal which they thought was the best for me. And I was so angry and heart-broken that I said yes to it without a second thought." I was listening shocked.

"I have got engaged to that girl last month and we would be getting married next month. I do not know what to do." He paused again.

"Everything is finalized now. My parents will not agree to our marriage now. The societal image and their word to the girl's family is everything for them. There's another person involved. She is a good girl. You have to understand, Aarohi. It's too late now. I am so sorry. I am so sorry."

I could not control my tears. "You were right Rudra when you said that one day I will want to marry but you would have other plans. That day has come. I just didn't know how I would feel that day; now I do. I wish you all the happiness....all the happiness in the world. Good Bye Forever." My sobs couldn't let me say anything more.

I declared my love to the only guy I loved and all I got was a deep pain in my heart. Suddenly my legs weren't enough to support me and I grabbed the corner of the table on which the phone was placed. There was no going back on this. I knew I had lost him again, this time forever.

Heartbroken I was. I could feel the heaviness in my throat. I felt bodiless two hands chocking my heart.

Little did I know about my own heart. The pain was nothing but love that was flowing in my veins. It was tearing my soul and stabbing my mind.

I had never felt like this before. It was a feeling of heart break, a feeling of loss of trust, a feeling of disbelief in what was happening. I was sad as well as angry over Rudra's decision. When you love someone too much the thought of losing them becomes unacceptable.

A severe headache was tearing my nerves. Tears rolled down my eyes. I hated it when my anger took the form of tears. But it's hard to suppress your emotions sometimes. You lose control over your mind and eyes. At such times, you just want to reach a place where you don't have to hide from what you are feeling. To be with someone to whom you can express what you are going through. You just want someone to hug you tight, tell you everything will be alright. But my someone was gone forever.

There are situations in life which transform you, a permanent transformation which some people call 'Maturity' but it can better be called 'Loss of Innocence as well as Ability To Trust'. The best thing we can do is to learn from the life experiences and move on without speculating the results because every person we meet in life is different. Instead we should learn from situations we face in our lives and imbibe the best in our personalities.

We absorb the impacts of events of life around us. We learn, not only from ours but others' mistakes as well, but we also learn from others' good gestures and kindness. Everything that happens around us, positive or negative, leaves a mark on us. This influence may be small or big. We can attract the good as well as bad vibes and incorporate it in our personality. It all depends on our personality and attitude. Being in touch with our inner-self and absorbing the good around us helps to grow in life.

THE GREY SHADE

How do you classify a feeling that is neither a clear Yes nor a No. Neither a 'Black' nor a 'White'. The two extreme colors of Black and White are the acceptable colors but what about the Grey Shades of the complicated feelings.

There are a number of feelings which can't be expressed as being happy or sad. You may feel insecure or anxious when you actually are expected to be happy. Or may not feel sad in a situation where people expect you to be heartbroken.

Many a times we get baffled between our desires and what others expect from us. We chase the dreams which we are expected to chase by others. Sometimes we persuade ourselves to forget our actual desires and start chasing something which is expected and accepted by the individuals around us.

A feeling of heaviness in the heart is not always a heart attack, sometimes it's because our heart has been tied with other's expectations. It brings a feeling of unhappiness and helplessness. It feels like we are being forced to do what we do not really want to do in life. Why does this happen? Why do we let ourselves be burdened with other's expectations? Why do we deviate from our life path to fulfill what someone else is expecting us to do?

Many a times we do major things in life for pleasing others. Like choosing a career or life partner under parental pressure, having a baby under family and societal pressure, getting into things we do not like under peer pressure etc. This only leads to malaise and vexation later on and we repent afterwards because of such decisions.

These crushed feelings rise and express themselves at wrong time. Actual happiness resides in doing things which we actually want to do and true sadness also arises when we are unable to achieve what we actually desired. Life is too short to carry the burden of others' desires and forget about own self in the process.

CHAPTER 5

I was struggling with myself. *Heart break is a struggle of loving yourself more than loving someone else.* The thought of Rudra getting married to someone else was breaking me internally. I kept to myself and lost appetite so rarely went to mess.

"What are you doing awake this late?" Amita asked as she entered my room one night and caught me gazing up at the wall.

It was 3 A.M. and I was still awake.

"Nothing. Just trying to sleep. But why are you awake?" I asked her.

"I just got up to go to the loo and thought of checking on you. What is wrong Aarohi? Just let it go, naa...." She said sitting beside me on my bed.

"I am trying, yaar. I do not know why I am becoming an insomniac and whatever time I sleep I see weird dreams."

"What weird dreams?" Amita asked worried.

"I dream of being alone in the forest wailing for help, falling from the terrace of a high building, of being drowned in deep waters. I know something is really wrong with me. I just cannot get hold of me and my emotions." I said. Tears of helplessness were now rolling down my eyes.

"Save me yaar. Save me. I feel I am becoming more depressed and insomniac day by day and I do not know what to do. I want to be the same person that I was earlier.

Help me." I was sobbing now.

"You will be fine Aarohi. I know it is a tough phase, but it is not everlasting." Amita hugged me and wiped my tears.

"Okay. Enough now. Get up and come with me. I will not let you be alone at this time. You sleep in my room today. My roommate has gone home. Sleep on her bed." Amita held my hand pulling me to get up. I got up and followed her to her room.

I was in an emotional turmoil and no matter what I did or not did; my mind was always busy in thinking one thing- 'What if..?'

"What if I would have realized earlier? I should have. I should have known what I felt. I was not even sure of my own feelings for so long. How?..." I kept on repeating thoughts in my mind, knitting scenarios where I could have ended up with Rudra. *Mind is a well of thoughts; but you rarely get the thought you want.*

I knew that I was going through a difficult phase in life; a fight for myself, with myself. When there is conflict within you, you do not know what to do. *When soul craves for something, but life has other plans, you are the one who pays the price with those feelings.* When things are not in your control, you start to question everything. Everything, even the smallest tasks, become a problem. Your life appears to be at a standstill.

As Amita had advised me, I too was trying to console myself that every phase passes even the toughest ones. Sometimes waiting for the right time is the best option.

Things which are bound to happen will happen, but at the right time. So, we should do our best and then surrender ourselves to destiny and let life find its own route. To live your life to the fullest, everyone needs to go through its different conflicts. You need to experience different situations, feel different emotions and come out of difficult scenarios. Life is a struggle at every stage. Sometimes, we enjoy the grapple and become passionate to accomplish what we want while sometimes it feels like being trapped under deep water, failing to catch the breath. You may have thoughts that this is the end. But then you gather yourself, struggle hard and survive. This is life.

Theory of "Survival Of The Fittest" by Charles Darwin states that only the fittest and the one with power of acclimatization survives the ordeal of world. The one who struggles and does not give up survives and only those individuals know the true sense of progressing in life. I needed to take this struggle positively.

Broken heart, broken wings and still you fly. Life's blows make you staunch and you sustain to fly higher.

With such thoughts I tried to gather back myself and be normal. But the only place I could think of to relieve me of this pain was my mother's embrace. I would feel less pain when I was with my mother. The world seemed a better place. I realized that I have to get hold of myself else I would end up getting more dejected and lose myself. Mom would try to console me and make me understand that struggle is the part of life, and struggling is a good sign and everything that happens in our life has something good in store for us.

When we struggle with our own limitations, our own fears, it means we are trying to evolve and no matter how much evolved we are, there is always a scope of improvement. We can never be perfect. But only those who struggle in life are the ones who keep growing and become better person day by day.

"Aarohi, just understand one thing. Life doesn't give you everything you want, but if you are fair to yourself, fare to your life and true to your feelings; your life does give you what's best for you. Nobody gets problems more than what they can handle, kid; but we need our strength to do that. This is the struggle of your life and one day...far off from today, may be tomorrow...I don't know when; but kid, one day, you will know what you want. Till then just keep your patience. Keep yourself happy."

"Only those who go through pain know how it feels and can understand the agony of others. It is the struggle that they go through when in pain which makes them evolved and empathetic enough to understand others' sitch. The adversities in life are the wonderful opportunities in disguise for your growth. You just need to en-cash them the right way. Life is a hard teacher sometimes, but what it teaches should always remain with us and should help us in our ultimate aim i.e. personal growth. Living your life and also understanding the life from someone else's viewpoint is important for you to evolve as a human being. This is possible only when you are ready for the change and face the different circumstances life throws at you boldly."

"I understand this, mom. But I know myself too. I know that my heart would take some time to heal. *Some sufferings cannot be expressed. When you lose something you never had, you feel the pain every moment.*" I said emotionally. "I know, mom, I sound like every other heartbroken teenager, may be even worse, but I feel something changed, mom. Changed forever."

"Aarohi, you said it yourself; give it time, kid. Give it time." Mom was sad looking at me, understanding my meaning. "Even the people who are the most powerful or the richest have their certain wishes unfulfilled; things which they cannot control and are bound to be left to the almighty god and their destiny."

I listened and understood what mom said. "You are right mom. I need to focus on what is important to me in life, the things I wanted to achieve from the very beginning. I just need to fight with my inner conflicts and win over them. I very well understand that if you really want something and try to achieve it with all your strength, heart and soul, nothing can stop you from getting it. I need to make a choice as to what is important to me and what I actually want. I need to get hold of myself and fight the thoughts and inhibitions which are holding me back."

I was trying hard. But moving on, is not that easy. I succumbed to the pit again and again. It takes its due course. Rightly said, 'It's easier to fall out of love only when you don't want to.'

I came back to hostel. Life took its pace again. But for me, the pace was lost. I often remained lost in my thoughts, blaming myself.

CHAPTER 6

I was more focused towards my studies now. Somehow, I wanted to find peace by burying myself in work. I wanted to work so hard that there was no time left for the memories to cloud my mind. I wanted to run away from all the memories that tried to haunt me. But still at the end of the day I was never alone. I was surrounded with the memories of Rudra. I kept thinking about the good times I spent with Rudra, repent of not being able to realize my love earlier, the moment I talked to Rudra for the last time made me cry in alone and the thought of Rudra being married to someone else killed me inside. Everybody around me knew how I felt and tried cheering me up, but to no avail.

"Aarohi, open the door." Amita's voice brought me back from my reverie to present.

Amita was knocking the door of my room. I got up and opened the door.

"What happened? Why are you so excited?"

"You have been allotted a roommate and she is your acquaintance too"

"Who is it?"

"Ravneet. She will be your roommate. The warden just told me about it."

I was glad to know this. Ravneet was my friend but was a day scholar. She had lost her parents in an accident a few months back and was going through the toughest time of her life. She was earlier staying with her family but now she needed to shift to the hostel.

I had always liked Ravneet but did not get to interact with her much as I was mostly with my hostel friends and day scholars had a separate group of their own. But whenever I did, I felt her to be a quiet, calm and charming girl. She was really good in her studies as well.

By the evening, Ravneet brought her luggage and other stuff to my room. I was happy to have her as roommate. But I felt very sorry for Ravneet's circumstances. Losing parents in such a small age is devastating.

Days were passing and I was getting to know her more and slowly we were becoming good friends. I was amazed to see the patience and tranquility Ravneet had. She was mostly smiling and no one could imagine that she was going through such emotional turmoil in her life. I felt my own sorrow so little in front of her grief.

"How can you be so calm and smiling? I am so amazed to see your strength. How do you deal with such big emotional loss that life has thrown at you?" I asked Ravneet one evening while chit chatting.

Ravneet sighed and replied "When I had lost my parents, my whole world was devastated. I had lost the most important people in my life, the ones because of whom I did not have to worry about anything. Everything I needed was them. Suddenly, my world changed and I did not know what to do. No one is prepared for such things to happen in life."

"I also had my share of sleepless nights. I used to curse myself for not being with my parents when they needed me, I thought of the things I could have done to save them which I could not do at right time. I used to remember the small incidents when I annoyed my mother, when she was hurt because of me. I used to remember everything and wept for days and nights. Then one day I saw my mother in my dream. I could feel as if she was there in reality. She was sitting by my side while I was sleeping. She put her hand on my forehead lovingly like she did when she was alive. Then she called my name and said. "Forgive Yourself." She kissed me and got up to leave. I wanted to stop her and I woke up from my dream. But there was a change in me, I suddenly had forgiven myself of the guilt I had. I was at peace; my mind was calm. I do not know how, but I understood what those two words she said meant. What she meant."

She continued, "I know why it is so hard to forgive ourselves? Sometimes, we find it easier to forgive others but we fail at forgiving ourselves. There are situations in life which do not turn out as expected. Since our mind is so much conditioned for things to turn out as we want, we are unable to accept the truth and start considering ourselves responsible for the failure. We keep carrying the load of this guilt in our conscience."

"We may seem normal and happy to the world but deep inside we burn in our own guilt. Everything becomes lifeless because we are not able to accept and consider ourselves as normal human who can err, who cannot predict things and who is not responsible for all the reasoning and the surprises life has in store for us."

"The things which happen to us are carried with us throughout our life, changing our personalities and the perception of the world from time to time which are called our life-experiences. It is the entire load we carry on our mind just like carrying a sack full of unwanted things on the back. We carry this baggage of emotions and self-blaming with us."

I listened to her astonished. I couldn't utter a word. I felt as if the reasons were different, but our pain was same. Our feelings were same.

"It's just that we forget to be kind to ourselves, to expect less from ourselves and end up becoming a person which we never were. We need to remember that whatever we do in a situation at a particular time is the best we could do. Whether we do it with all the thinking and wisdom or not, it would have been the best thing to happen at that time. So, we should not regret about it." She smiled.

"We always try to do the best that we can so why to blame yourself later on, Aarohi. The way I did my best, you too did the best you could do. Rudra was not meant to be yours; he played his role in your life. He made you aware of the feeling of love. Now his role is over in your life. Just let things play out, what's supposed to happen will happen. We don't have to carry the blame and load on our souls."

"Don't forgive yourself for anybody else. *Forgive, for your own happiness. Forgive, for your own peace. Forgive, because you do not deserve a burnt soul and a fuming mind.* And once we learn to forgive ourselves and not to over-think the issues, life becomes easier. Then why not practice it and live life as it is destined to be. *Let go of everything you are trying to hold on to. Let go of the things that have the power to break you. Open the tight fists of your mind. Just let go and thank God for this beautiful life."*

I kept staring at Ravneet's face, astonished and emotional. In a flash, I ran the two steps between us and hugged her. I hugged her tight and let myself go. Tears were glistening from my eyes and something powerful than I ever felt, a strong dam broke down in me and I started crying. I cried and cried in the arms of Ravneet, who hugged me back tight and firm. She too had tears in her eyes. I cried as I remembered Rudra's final words, his face, his smile and his wedding picture that I saw a few days back; courtesy to ever growing social media. I had no idea how long I kept hugging Ravneet, but when I let go, I felt lighter in myself. I felt as if some ice that froze my heart had melted and washed away in tears and I could feel things again.

"I am sorry."

"Don't be. You will be fine, Aarohi. We are friends, we will remain so."

I smiled as I felt so proud of my friend. I felt highly inspired by her so much wise words at this young age. I was no longer sad and had understood that I need to free myself of the guilt and burden that I carried on my soul. Slowly tears started flowing off my eyes. But inside I felt a different kind of lightness. I was liberated. I forgave myself.

TAKE YOUR TIME

Life happens at its own pace. As we grow up, we realize that we should let things happen as they are. Some things cannot be controlled by us. But what we can control is to free ourselves of our own expectations. Let life take its course.

It could be a goal one wants to achieve. Keep trying; you may achieve it later than others. But an effort in the right direction surely bears fruit. Some may soar in life early while in some cases it may take time. Take your time without comparison with others. You are unique and so is your destiny.

It could be a heartbreak, which we may feel is irrecoverable. Just be gentle with yourself. Give yourself the desirable time. Every heart recovers at its own pace and the strongest hearts have the deepest scars. Let yourself be sad. Allow yourself to be happy too. Don't hold on to any emotion. Let it flow. An emotionally sensitive person should not consider being sentimental as a negative trait. It's a gift by god to feel the flavor of every emotion more than others, to be empathetic and to live life in true sense. Be proud to be what you are.

There may be something which is related to someone's sentiments or may be a truth which one knows or may be the mind knows but the heart does not accept. Just let life happen as it is. It will be accepted by your heart one day. Time heals everything and prepares you to accept truth slowly. Do not strain yourself about the issue. A day will come when you would accept the truth and face it boldly.

Life is like a road. We need to reach the other end of the road in all situations. In every situation, we achieve something at the cost of other. Just like we may speed up our vehicle and reach the end of road early but at the cost of burning more fuel and stressing the engine. In life, we may overstrain ourselves and compromise our mental health to be at a desired position in life early. It is for us to see as to what is important to us in the long run of this short life.

As rightly said by Friedrich Nietzsche "And those who were seen dancing were thought to be insane by those who could not hear the music".

CHAPTER 7

I was no longer sad and taciturn. I had accepted the reality. Some people inspire you to the core. Ravneet was one of those in my life. I decided to take my life as it comes. I started getting back to my normal self and focus on my dreams. I had two dreams, one a challenge and the other my heartfelt desire. First, I want to excel in my field of study, to be a scientist and pursue a career in it. Second, I want to travel the world and explore life by visiting different places and meeting different people.

At the hostel, Ravneet, Amita and me became really good friends, sticking to each other through all thick and thin. Now it was all three of us hanging out together in college campus, mess and outside. Life was on its track finally.

Time was flying and I was working harder than ever. While I was focused on my entrance exam which was the first stepping stone for my dream of getting into Ph.D., Amita and Ravneet were preparing to move out of India for further studies.

The zeal to accomplish my first dream was back. I liked to succeed the right way. I always loved to put in efforts to learn something. It seems like a small victory and has its own charm. I know that these small victories were bringing me closer to my dream. As the date of entrance exam came nearer, I had started spending most of the time at college library rather than spending at the hostel.

I worked diligently, put in extra efforts but I enjoyed the feeling when I scored better than others and was giving a tough competition to the topper of the class. Apart from good grades, I tried to keep my focus on learning because that was ultimately going to help me throughout life.

The eagerness to learn should never end as it is the sign of an alive soul. Even the concept of learning is not limited to the books or reading. Opportunities to learn present themselves every now and then in our lives. But it all depends on our attitude whether we grasp it or not. This is similar to our learning at school. Some students learn rather than just cramming it up as it is. This makes them excel in the exams because they actually gain knowledge through learning. The attitude starts forming from the childhood itself.

Life also offers us things to learn through experiences. Some are hard experiences while some are soft. But every experience teaches us something. Some people learn from their as well as the experiences of others and try to inculcate the best in their lives. While there are others who keep on repeating similar mistakes throughout their life but never learn. It all depends on our outlook towards life.

I knew where I could fail to keep pace with my ambition. I knew that I would have to face hardships to clear the exam, but I was prepared for all challenges. I knew that nothing could stop me now as I had started to work with my heart, mind and soul towards one goal. My biggest goal for now was of getting selected for Ph.D., my first step towards my ambition to be a scientist.

LEARN

Life is not a race where you need to compare your life with others and compete to be ahead of them. Life is like an exam where everyone has a different question paper and need to answer it as per their own learning. People who compare their lives to others and mold it accordingly, never come out as winners.

Your attitude towards life determines its worthiness. It's similar to a situation where you have a disagreement with your fellow colleague and you are discussing it. Here, you can have two types of attitudes i.e. to discuss or to argue. When you argue, you try to prove your point without any intension to learn from situation. But when you discuss things, you take the other one's point of view into consideration and the outcome is learning. You may be right but still you learn one thing or the other.

When you develop this attitude in life, you never fail. Whenever you fall, you learn and you get up stronger, wiser. Such people are the toughest ones because they never fail in any situation. They extract the maximum out of any situation, the life puts them into. They become the true winners as they try to continuously evolve in life.

"Try and try again, till you succeed" is an old proverb that everybody learns in the childhood itself. However, in addition to it, efforts in the right direction are also important. If you try again and again in wrong direction, repeating the same mistakes, you are never going to succeed in your goals. Here, your attitude to learn comes into play. In order to know where you went wrong, you need to have the attitude and patience to learn from the situations you face so that you do not repeat same mistakes and align your efforts in right direction.

In order to develop the attitude to learn, one of the most fundamental things to inculcate in your personality is the patience to listen.

We may notice that the people who are successful in life are very good listeners. This is one of the most important factors which contributes to their success and helps to maintain the level of success throughout their life.

We meet many people in life, who love to speak but do not listen. Also, there are people who hear what you say but actually do not listen. There is a difference in "Hearing" and "Listening". When you hear things, it involves your ears and you hear things without any intension to understand and learn. But while listening, your ears, mind and heart are focusing on the thing the other person is saying. Here, you try to understand as well as learn. These virtues of listening make it an indivisible part of learning and growth.

CHAPTER 8

Time passed on its pace. Slowly the course was on the end. It was time to bid goodbye to Amita and Ravneet who were leaving India and going to Canada. Although, they were going to different cities in Canada for pursuing different courses but they could manage to meet each other on weekends and were happy about it.

"Our lives are going to be changed. I am feeling quite anxious. Though I am happy to see my dreams getting fulfilled, but at the same time leaving you here and going off to Canada feels weird, you know?" Amita and me were standing in the hostel balcony and looking at the road, talking and recalling those memories we shared.

I hugged Amita emotionally. I had spent both delightful and gloomy moments of my life with Amita and could easily sense that I would never find a friend like her again.

"Change is a part of life Amita. Everything changes and nothing is permanent." I looked into her eyes. She too had tears in them. "Would you call me from Canada?"

"Are you stupid? Why will I call you? Don't you know that ISD call rates are so high?" Amita laughed teasingly.

"Who will you call then? Subhan Allah?" I asked joking.

"Areyy... You know the news?" She suddenly sounded excited.

"Subhan Allah's boyfriend took that diamond ring back from her."

"Really? Why?"

"Don't know. I heard that he broke-up with her."

"Ohh... Why?"

"Don't know the reason. Heard it from someone. May be he finally realized that she looks like a goat from the side."

We both started laughing.

"This is mean Amita. You are so evil to her. I am sure you will be happy now. Poor girl... She is going through heartbreak." I felt sympathetic for her.

"Don't be so serious, yaar. You know her, na? She was drunk for two days and now she is fine. You will see her with a new boyfriend in some days. Note down my words." She said lightly.

"On a serious note..." Amita's voice grew serious and authority filled. "Promise me one thing, Aarohi. Rudra and his chapter in your life will not stop you. You will move ahead and find that love in your life. I am not giving any instructions on your studies and goals and any other thing because you are meant to get them and you will get them in half time with your pace. But I love you, you are my friend, Aarohi, and you promise me you will give everything in this life a chance to grow. You will not fear anything... not even love."

I smiled back; but my eyes had tears. I knew Amita wanted the best for me, but this one thing I couldn't promise her.

"Dadi amma, go open a dating service, I tell you. Amita, I am just gonna let life happen, okay?"

She didn't sound much happy with the answer but she let go. She hugged me tight and we silently looked off the hostel balcony; last time together.

I knew that Amita would miss me too. After all we had spent the best of our times together which we were going to miss throughout our lives. All the emotional phases of life that we spent together brought us so close to each other. We were each other's confidantes. She always wanted the best in my life. But even I didn't have all the answers to my life, so how could I promise them to her.

Amita was leaving the hostel early. Her course in Canada was due early. Her family arrived to take her home. I met them and bid Amita Good-Bye with a heavy heart. 'Don't know when I am going to meet this stupid girl again in this life.' I was sad. Moving on still wasn't my forte, but I was managing. This was the phase of big changes in my life.

Ravneet too left in a few days. Her departure wasn't any less emotional. She was happy that she was getting so much scholarship to study as her family, as much she had, and supports were limited. Hostel was becoming quiet slowly as students were leaving. My batchmates were leaving for their respective future aims with dreams in their eyes. There was silence in the hostel for most part of the day, until someone's parents arrived and another person leaves forever.

CHANGE

Change means moving ahead, change means growth. It is the necessity of life. Most times changes make us sad, because we become habitual of living our lives in a particular manner and do not want to come out of our comfort zone. It could be an emotional attachment, change in nature of job, change in place of living. We are sometimes scared to leave our comfort zones and proceed ahead in life. It is human nature. But all the changes in life should be taken positively as they store the best of our future. They store the future itself.

We may feel disheartened initially when it happens but with time we realize the importance of those changes eventually. A kid who starts going to school cries on first few days when leaving for school. He hates the change and tries his best to make his parents give up the idea of sending him to school. But the parents know the importance of this change in his life.

God behaves like our parent in our destiny. He knows what is best for us. We may have to face hardships initially but when we reach our desired goals, we feel thankful to God for taking hard decision for us. The kid too realizes the importance of going to school when he grows up, fulfills his dreams and becomes independent.

But just like parents can help us in our life only up to some extent, God only helps those who put efforts to fulfill their dream. As it is said that you can bring a horse near water but you cannot make him drink it. It's the horse who has to desire and put his effort in the end. The changes that take place in our life depend on our thoughts and efforts. We cannot solely depend on God to make us reach our destiny.

Changes in our lives are a sign of the direction in which our life is moving. We can change the direction by being the in-charge of our life and driving the vehicle of our life our own way. This can be done only when you are clear about your goals. Else when you are just living and moving in the direction where the crowd is going, you leave your life directionless, aimless to the fate.

Many times, people do things just for the sake of doing it, to follow what everyone does in the society, not following what their heart and mind says. This way we delay the changes that were meant for us to happen in our destiny.

Sometimes, we get too delayed by following the societal norms and the crowd that our life changes its direction permanently and we start to follow the path we were never meant to follow. This leads to the dissatisfaction in our lives and our soul craves again and again to correct the path which, in us, is reflected as anxiety, stress or unhappiness in doing our jobs. But till that time, we are so much trapped in our established life that it seems impossible to go back and we prefer to ignore our inner voice. Many people live their life like that and the sad part is that they do not actually live their life.

CHAPTER 9

I kept working hard and studying even more. My heart was set on the entrance exam for my Ph.D. and I wanted to crack that exam anyhow. I was sleeping less, doing almost nothing but studying. My mind was set on the goal that I had to achieve. Finally, I appeared for the entrance exam and cleared it.

"Hello, Dr. Aarohi. Congratulations." My sister Aakriti had called me up. We were that kind of siblings who rarely talked but still were never disconnected. The siblings' connection is rock solid.

"Thanks sis. There is still time for using this prefix." I replied happily.

"Arey. It's almost sure now. You are getting into doctorate course. I am so happy for you."

"Yes. But the real journey is just about to begin and it is not an easy one. You know na, I have always been interested into field of research in Cancer specifically Breast Cancer. I wish I get to complete my research under Mr. Ojha. He is such a treasure trove of knowledge in this field. Just trying for that now."

"I know you will successfully do whatever you want to do in life. I have this gut feeling you know. Don't worry about that. You just tell me when are you coming home next. Let's meet up. It has been long we haven't met."

"Yes. I will plan soon. Bye." I said as we hung up.

After completing masters, it's a grapple to make your

mark at a young age of twenty-two. You want to be maverick, take care of your finances and follow what you wished to do. Fighting the competitive exams and clearing it, I paved my way to make my dream partial reality, getting into doctorate.

When you achieve the dreams seen with open eyes, it opens the minds of many around us. You become an inspiration for others too. Everything was going on as per my plan. It seemed life had finally started to bloom and Mr. Ojha too consented to be my guide.

Sitting in front of the big cabin, waiting for my turn to meet Mr. Ojha, I was excited about my first day as a research scholar. I always hoped I could make a good impression on the first day itself.

"Good Morning Sir" I entered the room and wished Mr. Ojha.

It was an adorned room; decorated mostly with the books as one would expect a scholar's room to be. But the whole collection consisted of most famous reads from almost every field. It suggested that he loved to read. So, did I. The books in the room were fascinating me. There was a period piece clock hanging on the wall in front of his worktable which must have reminded him of the time (that's really what clocks are meant to do), as his days were mostly packed with meetings and lectures.

"Good Morning and welcome to you. It's the beginning of your new academic journey, a journey that you will very well remember throughout your life." replied Mr. Ojha smiling and adjusting his spectacles. Mostly, he just seemed a bit busy with some paperwork.

"Sir, what work would I be doing in Ph.D.?" I asked.

"Well you need to find that out. I can guide you accordingly."

He always checked thoroughly work done by the potential students before taking them in, so he must be aware of my work as well. He must have known I had the potential, that's why I was standing in his office. It was famous for him that he only took in students who he thought had enough potential that he should devote time on them. Maybe he wanted me to explore things myself and give me the freedom to decide the line of my research.

"Sir, in how many years can I expect my Ph.D. to be completed?" I asked the question which was hovering over my mind since many years.

He smiled and looked at me kindly. "It all depends on you and your attitude. You can complete Ph.D. in as early as three years too but it can take many years if your attitude and approach is not right, Aarohi."

I was going through a mixture of emotions that day. I was happy and sure of myself. But I was nervous as well as very emotionally on edge.

Mr. Ojha then took out a few articles published in various journals and handed over to me. "You can go through these articles and decide the work you would like to do. You can start by visiting the laboratory and get to know about the work going on by your seniors. I have 3 research scholars working with me at present. You can meet them to know their work. They can also guide you with the basic techniques and processes. You take your time to decide your topic of research and meet or call me whenever you have any doubt or issue. I think that will be good for now?" He was bemused, but polite. He must have become habitual to the overwhelming responses of the new students.

"Thank you, sir," I replied and decided to see the laboratory. I placed the articles in my bag and moved towards the lab with great enthusiasm and a Nobel laureate ideas and expectations.

I was delighted and kept on thinking of getting 'Ph.D. within three years' and imagining telling the same to Aakriti, unaware of the fact that the coming years were going to be a swedge for me which were going to change me forever.

The lab was quite huge with all the apparatus and instruments needed for the research. One of the walls was divided into sections and had different cabinets which had many chemicals and various glassware needed for experiments. I saw two people engrossed with their work in the lab, a girl and a boy. I felt the scholar and academic vibes of the room. I was excited but also a bit nervous, but mostly I was enthusiastic to be able to start my Ph.D. I wanted to know everything and meet everyone around; asking them questions and seeing everything in the lab. I went to my seniors, smiling and thinking that I would learn something from them.

"Hi, mam, I am Aarohi. I have joined today only, for my Ph.D. under Mr. Ojha." I went to the girl working in the lab. "You must be my senior here."

"Hello, Aarohi. I am Nidhi." She said with a forced smile.

'She didn't seem very happy to meet me. Maybe she had her own troubles which were bothering her.' I thought and chose to ignore Nidhi's behavior.

"Mam, I am trying to figure out the topic of my work in Ph.D. I haven't decided on anything yet and that's making me nervous. What is your topic of research?" I asked.

However, Nidhi gave a very vague and short reply which was of no use to me in deciding my area of work. She seemed like not interested in talking to me much and kept hinting of work.

I didn't talk to her further as Nidhi seemed very disinterested in answering my queries. This, however, did not affect me too much. I was engrossed in my own thoughts of realizing my dream. The first day to this lab, everything new happening to me these days was proving to be such a high point in my life, as I had never had. Of course, I knew that it was a start to many more such days in my life. Nonetheless, I was euphoric, and wanted to remain so. I was an achiever and I knew that I was going to achieve my dream one day. I was not going to give up on my dream because of anything. I had entered into this field with the aim of not only completing my Ph.D. but also to contribute to the betterment of mankind through my work. I wanted to return to this university and the society who were giving me the chance to fulfill my dreams.

I spent the day sitting in the lab and going through the articles given to me by Mr. Ojha. I also met my other seniors; Ankit and Shailendra. They were coming and going into the lab and were busy with their work. I interacted a bit with them too and had a realization that journey of Ph.D. was not going to be an easy ride for me. "Struggle is the spice of life, Aarohi." I was reminded of my mother's words.

'Yes, more spice is always needed.' I thought and smiled at my thought.

"Would you like to join me for lunch?" asked Ankit. He was going to the canteen.

"Thank you. Some other day, may be. I was just leaving for the hostel to have my lunch." It was Friday and one of my other favorites 'Kadhi Chawal' was on the menu for the day. I happily started walking towards the hostel to relish my favorite food.

The sight of that yummy treat of Kadhi Chawal on the mess table was good enough to make me forget my worries. I sat on the chair to have food and looked at the chair opposite to mine. My mind suddenly was filled with thoughts of Amita. But she was not there. I missed her very much. It was not that I had never eaten food alone in mess. But the thought of having food alone without a 'who will have more kadhi-pakodis?' contest with Amita was making me sad. I was habitual of being alone in past few days, but I missed Amita and Ravneet a lot. I decided to call them soon. I started having lunch and realized, 'Kadhi Chawal' lost just a small amount of charm for me.

DARE TO DREAM

Dreams mean different things to different people, but mostly they do include one common detail for everyone. That is to be able to prove something in front of everyone. Yes, this may be considered as flaunting, but the truth is that; whenever we dream of something we actually think of people standing around us when we realize our dream. People like our family, who would be happy and proud of us. People like our friends, who will pat our backs. People like normal people we see daily, who will look at us in awe.

Dr. Kalam said "Dream isn't the one we have while sleeping. It's the one that doesn't let us sleep."

Having a dream is the most important thing in life. To dream and to live that dream, to be able to fulfill it is not necessarily an easy task. Sometimes it is so difficult that people give up. Only few have the courage and determination to dream and work hard to realize it. Too many rules and regulations exist which knock you down and make you feel like quitting. That's when the patience is tested.

When you follow your passion, your dream, the path becomes as beautiful as the destination itself. This is what you want to do, this is what you want to achieve. When you focus on the hardships of the path too much, you want to quit. When you focus on the destination too much, you want to quit as well. The key to it is to focus on both things in a balance. When you feel your way is very hard to move on, look at the destination you planned for yourself. But when the destination feels long way to go, focus on the way that you have covered or are covering. This will help you stick to your path as well as your dream.

Our heart talks to us from time to time. It tells us the things which are good for us; it warns us too which we sometimes call intuition. We just need to listen to it. Many a times, we choose to ignore what our heart says. We choose to take our decisions based on our other priorities and ignore the inner voice.

When we make it a habit to ignore our heart's voice always, it too starts talking to us lesser and we lose touch with our inner voice. Having your heart, soul and mind in sync with one another is a tough thing to achieve and those who master it believe that everything resides within us. There is nothing that we cannot achieve. We just need to believe in ourselves.

The greatest belief in the world is the belief in oneself. We look outside to see the belief. We want our parents, friends, loved ones to believe in us while the truth is that till the time we do not believe in ourselves, no one else will actually believe in us. When we believe in ourselves and proceed towards our goal with determination and hard work, success is guaranteed and it's a world proven fact that everyone believes in a successful person. To win the belief of people we care about we need to believe in ourselves and everything follows inevitably.

Do not die before your death. Killing one's dreams does have that effect on people. Most people die many times in their life when they try to kill their true selves by believing in people who discourage them from believing in themselves. People feel safe to be part of the crowd. Doing what others do, following what others believe and always trying to fit in the group where they feel safe in their minds. This lessens the danger of getting judged on one's beliefs. But the question arises, 'if you believed in it, why were you not ready to be judged upon it?'

As it has been quoted by someone beautifully, "I will never fit in; this is one of my best qualities". It is actually true. We are not made to fit in; we are not made to follow each other like herds. Every human being is made unique by god. And he needs to explore himself. By trying to copy others, we disrespect our true self; we ignore our inner voice and our true feelings.

You feel the real joy when you strive to achieve the goal against all odds, when you prove yourself to the world. As action speaks louder than words, we need to put forth our actions. Believing in yourself and fulfilling your goals. It brings a satisfaction of answering the world with action rather than mere words. When you understand yourself, you are not worried to understand the world anymore. You find all strengths, solution to the problems and clarity on path to be followed within you. Never give up listening to your heart, your inner-voice and believe in yourself.

CHAPTER 10

I had selected the topic to work on in my Ph.D., but I was still struggling with some scientific terms that I had not heard before. I searched for my queries on internet and got more confused. I was trying hard to understand the work and decide the topic for pursuing my doctorate.

While trying to understand the work in detail, I was simultaneously trying to learn new techniques and protocols for the lab; I felt would be helpful to me in future. I got chance to interact mostly with Nidhi, who was always reluctant to help me and getting anything worthy out of her mouth was a big task in itself. I always tried to be polite and nice to her. However, Nidhi felt my coming into the lab being a burden and was worried about sharing the available consumables, chemicals and materials which she didn't want to share.

Ankit was mostly nice to me. He joined one year back and that made him my senior, but I did not like him much. Something just always let me off him. I got the image that Ankit was just interested in superficial chats and wasn't as deep in his heart as he sometimes showed off. I just couldn't feel on the same page with him; that made me avoid him as much as possible. But mostly somewhere in my heart, I knew that Ankit liked me more than normal and that made me anxious. I felt really uncomfortable around him feeling that he was over-crowding me.

"I saw you on morning walk today. I, too, am an early riser. We can go for morning walk together if you like" Ankit asked one fine day working in the lab.

"No, you are mistaken. You must have seen someone else. I don't go for morning walks. Never had, never will. I love my sleep too much." I lied, conveniently. I wasn't at all interested in going for my walks with Ankit.

He laughed and said, "You are trying to avoid me. Aren't you?"

I smiled and said, "No way. The last time I woke up early morning was when I was born. I never woke up early morning after that."

Ankit sensed the sarcasm in my voice and laughed. Ankit mostly talked about things not related to work. He seemed to be over-friendly to me and I did not find any compatibility with him. For me, it was easier to avoid him rather than talking to him on anything.

"Six months passed in understanding things around and I started my work gradually. I learnt many lab techniques that were going to help me in future. By now, for me, my Ph.D. has become like a baby to me; my own baby who I have to take care of, nurture and bring up the right way." I was lost in thoughts waiting for Mr. Ojha in his room.

He was a busy man but managed his time quite well. I was amazed by his time management skills and cool attitude. I never saw him panicked and was totally inspired by his patience.

"What are you thinking, Aarohi?" Mr. Ojha smiled while entering the room. He always took care of his students well, made sure they were okay and not bothered enough to stop pursuing their dreams. This helped them keep on track.

"Nothing, sir, I was just thinking that when we decide to achieve a goal in life, we see only the goal and the joy that will come after accomplishing it. However, there are so many hardships to be faced in the path that we are unaware of till the actual journey starts. The path may be easy or tough, but it actually reveals itself when it really is started. We all listen to what our colleagues, friends even family tell us, but the truth is revealed only when we start walking on our own. May be because every one of us, our path is different and to a different destination, it just feels similar, but it never is."

"Very philosophical today, are we?" He smiled.

"Doctorate of philosophy." I replied smiling and in a bemused tone.

"True. True." He laughed. "Likewise it's also a universal truth Aarohi. When I, too, got into Ph.D. many years back, I had heard many stories from friends and seniors about how difficult it is to complete Ph.D. and have an acronym "Dr." in front of my name, but slowly I got to know the path to my journey which revealed itself slowly." He looked as if he was reliving those memories. "I too had to overcome some hurdles which may seem small from outside but can actually stand like a rock between you and your dream.

"You do not have to worry. I will try to help you wherever possible. I know I have my own confines. I need to give priority to the research scholars whose work is on the verge of completion. I too need to prioritize my job as a guide, but you will always get my guidance and support." He smiled again.

I sighed hearing this and was assured that I was not alone in my struggle.

In evening, sitting in balcony of the hostel room and sipping my tea, I was recollecting the events of the day. The view of the sun set brought peace to my mind and assured me that everything has an end. Sun also sets in the evening and my troubles are not permanent as well. One day I was going to smile remembering this time and be proud of myself to have survived it gracefully. I was thinking all this. Suddenly my phone rang. It was Amita. After so long I felt really happy in myself as I picked up.

CHAPTER 11

Days were rolling by, not much eventful. Ph.D. was becoming a routine to me and I was happy for it. The feeling of newness doesn't live too much. It's always the routine a person yearns for.

I was getting positive results in the lab experiments I was carrying out. Mr. Ojha was very happy with my work, but these days he was concentrating more on the senior batch students and their work as they were on verge of completing their Ph.D. I had everything ready in my mind, but work was proceeding very slowly. I would feel disheartened, but mostly I ignored the smirk on Nidhi's lips and pacified myself. 'This is human behavior of feeling a sense of proud on getting importance from one's bosses.'

The lab work was not easy. I needed to arrange the chemicals I needed to carry out the experiments, the sample and chemicals needed to be stored properly at proper temperatures and conditions. All experimental results depend on everything from using the accurate grades of chemicals, using them in accurate quantities, storage conditions of the samples and calibration of apparatus used and it being sterilized in the right manner. Even if there was a small deviation in procedure, the results could deviate; failing the entire project, whole effort as well as the money involved is wasted too.

"Aarohi, you need to be home soon, beta." mom called one evening and sounded really panicked over phone.

"Mom, you sound upset. Are you okay? And dad? What happened, mom?" I got worried.

"Aarohi, it's your Naani ji. She is not well. She is in a hospital, kid. Doctors are not very hopeful for her. You know how much she loves you. You have been her favorite grandchild. She looks for you when we go to meet her. I think you should come here. She isn't well enough to be able to make it." Mom replied in a low tone.

"Okay, mom. I will take the next bus." I said. I knew that my naani had not been well since a year, but the way my mother talked this time made me really impatient to get home. I took permission from Mr. Ojha and left for the hostel to pack my bags.

While travelling, my mind was dwelling on all the lovely memories of the childhood spent with my naani. Naani always loved me more than my cousins since I was a kid. My cousins always complained about it. She had seven grandchildren including me, Aakriti and my cousins, but she loved me the most and used to say "Aarohi, you are the most innocent child. How would you survive in this clever world?"

I would feel awkward on listening to this and would reply "Naani why do you always say this?" Naani would hug me lovingly.

I loved the food cooked by my naani specially the Potato-curd rice was my favorite. Of course naani made amazing Kadhi-Chawal and Gobhi-ke-Paranthe too, especially for me. I had talked to her on phone a few months back.

"Naani, I am missing your potato-curd rice so badly." And naani promised me to cook it for me when I visit her next time. All these memories were making me feel really sad. Lost in my thoughts I was continuously praying for my naani to get well soon.

"I am home mom. I will be leaving for hospital in sometime. You want me to bring something from home?"

I asked my mother who along with dad and Aakriti was at the hospital.

"No, Aarohi. You come soon. Your naani's condition has become critical and she wants to meet you." Mom was almost crying.

I hurriedly left for the hospital in an auto-rickshaw. In another half an hour I was at the hospital. I inquired about the directions of ICU at the reception and rushed towards the room where naani was. I hated to visit hospitals and the hospital smell, but presently I was least bothered about it.

"Naani, I am here." I said.

I was shocked to see naani's condition. She had become very weak. It was hard to recognize her as she had lost a lot of weight. It seemed as if she had aged ten years in just a year. I was feeling very emotional to see her in this condition. Naani gestured me to sit beside her. She did not seem to have the energy to talk. I went near her and sat on the edge of the bed, fearing of hurting naani.

I held naani's hand. Her weak hands had needle and cannula fitted in them. Naani was looking at me lovingly.

"I am so happy you came. I was waiting only for you it seems. My time has come, Aarohi." she whispered in croaked voice.

"No, naani. Don't say this, naani." I had tears in my eyes.

"Do not cry, Aarohi. It had to happen one day and I am happy as well as ready to leave this world, but I am worried about you." She paused. "Aarohi, I am not able to speak much, but one important thing I want to tell you. *Do not forget who you are. Do not let the negative deeds of others effect you.* You keep doing good deeds and nothing bad will ever happen to you. You are my loving and innocent child. Always be good to others and every problem will resolve with time." Her voice was strained with breathlessness but she continued anyway. "Aarohi, you are different; different than this world and different than its habitants. You have to understand yourself before anyone else can. Try to listen to your heart because it's a good one and will never lie to you, beta."

"Naani, do not worry about me and I know you are not going anywhere."

"Aarohi, my child, do remember what I said and also be assured that my blessings are always with you, but I am sorry that I could not cook your favorite potato-curd rice for you."

I started crying hearing this. Naani was speaking with great difficulty now. The nurse standing nearby requested me to go out and let naani take rest.

"Aarohi beta, don't weep. Your naani lived a good life, but she has not been well and was in pain for quite some time now. It's time for her to get relieved from this pain. We had to face it one day." Mom said wiping my tears. I could see that her eyes were swollen. She had wept too.

I hugged her tight. "How could she be so strong?" I felt proud of my mother. "It is already ten on clock. You should go home, Aarohi. Only one visitor is allowed to stay at the hospital for the night. Dad and Aakriti are waiting for you outside to go home." Mom said releasing me from the hug.

"Okay, mom." I said getting hold of myself and left to go out.

After an hour, at eleven, I was serving food to dad when the phone at home rang. I ran to pick up the call as Aakriti had already gone to sleep in her room.

"Aarohi, your naani is no more, beta." Mom said with a heavy voice; trying to conceal her tears.

"We are coming mom." I replied not knowing how to react to this saddening news. Tears rolled down my eyes.

"We need to go to hospital, to bring naani." My face and tears said it all.

CHAPTER 12

I was grief-stricken. Everyone at home was, especially my mother, who had lost her own mother. However, she tried to be strong in front of me and Aakriti. For our sake, she kept her face with a small smile and kept on pacifying us about our naani's illness, but I had seen her weeping at night when everyone was sleeping. I could understand very well of her loss. She had all the right in the world to grieve over the loss of her mother. Loss of a parent is a grief like no other. I could understand all this because I saw the way Ravneet used to feel about her parents. It's like a roof that was protecting you, is taken away. It's a loss that runs deep and is irreparable. I however, did not go to console her because I knew that my mother would stop weeping on seeing me and would try to control her emotions. I wanted her emotions to flow and let her weep for her own peace. I was now able to understand life better. I decided to stay with my family for a few more days to help them in this period.

I was alone in house, one afternoon, and was sitting in my room when I felt someone was there outside. I went out to inquire about the source of the sound.

"Huh..." My breath fastened as I saw a person, exactly like naani, sitting on the bed in the room opposite to mine. I was shocked and scared. I tried to scream and opened my mouth, but no voice came. My breath was panting as I woke up with a start, mouth still open. I blinked my eyes and looked around, but I saw no one there.

"The dream seemed to be so real." I was thinking.

It was early morning. I looked around the house and saw that everyone was sleeping. I too went back to bed to sleep.

I was woken up again by ringing of my mobile phone. It was Ankit calling. 'Why is he calling me?' I murmured picking up the call.

"Hi, Aarohi. This is Ankit here."

"Hi, Ankit. Is everything okay?"

"Yes. Did I startle you? I am sorry. You okay?"

"Yeah. Sorry. Go ahead."

"Actually, I called you to give you this good news. Mr. Ojha asked me to convey the news to you." Ankit told the reason of his call.

"What good news?" I asked, curiously.

"The news you have been eagerly waiting for Aarohi. Your first paper has been accepted by the Science Journal and they will publish it in their next edition. Your work on breast cancer has been appreciated by them and they have requested to carry on the work further and keep them updated with your next research paper." Ankit told excitedly breaking the news to me.

"Really? Are you serious?" I asked happily. "Oh my God! I never thought I'd get this response."

I had submitted my research work to the science journal, but was not expecting them to take it seriously and publish it. Now, I was glad that I took the initiative of sending my research paper for publishing. I was going to be a published researcher now.

"Yes, Aarohi. I want a party this time and you cannot escape with a samosa party." He laughed.

"Yes, sure I will. Thanks for starting my day with this wonderful news. Bye." I said disconnecting the call.

This was such great news for me. I was relieved that my efforts were bearing fruits. I was reminded of my dream and was sure that my naani's blessings are there with me in facing every challenge. Also, I was reminded of the things naani said to me in hospital. "In all the chaos and worries of life it's hard to be good to everyone. Specially, when the people around you are always trying to pull your leg and creating hurdles for you, but I will always try my best to be good to everyone around me and would never alter my deeds because of other's behavior. Naani, I promise." I promised myself to no longer hold grudges against my seniors. I wanted to start afresh forgiving everyone and being myself.

I was back in my lab very soon. Mom was slowly returning to her routine. My leaves were over too and so I went back to college. My life was coming back to track. I had to order everything for next few days considering so much of work was piled up now.

"You had gone somewhere?" Nidhi asked.

"My maternal grandmother was not well so I had to go home." I replied.

"Oh. How is she now?" Nidhi asked.

"She is no more with us." I replied sadly.

"I am so sorry to know this." Nidhi said sympathetically. I did not how to respond so I kept quiet.

Nidhi was on the verge of completing experimental part of her Ph.D. She was getting positive results and was doing her research meticulously. She soon will be finished with it. I knew she had potential, even though she kept much to herself.

RIGHT PATH

Sometimes the right path becomes the toughest to walk. When we are young, we are more inclined to raw energy flowing in us and it becomes easy to speak the truth and follow the right path in life, but as we grow up, we realize that it is not as easy as it seems. People call it maturity or practicality to follow the grey path instead of white.

Many customs and religious ceremonies, which are followed by different groups of people keep on changing as per the region, beliefs and past practices. Many customs followed by the society seem to be wrong, illogical and opposing the law of equality of humans, but most people follow it any way no matter even if their heart says it is not right. It is because they have been so much accustomed with the belief of following their group and their beliefs that they have mastered the art of shutting the doors of their inner voice.

Sometimes, we try to fight for our point of view, but if we do not get support from others we try to convince our mind to let things be as they are. We know that the things happening to us are not morally right but when we look for support and fail to get it, we give up.

Many a times we stop pursuing the right path and choose the plain sailing one. Here, we try to convince ourselves that this is actually what we need and we avoid the challenges that we would face in the right path. We are just being practical by taking the easier path. We try to convince ourselves that the situation we are in is not as bad as we are thinking and we just need to adjust ourselves.

This is the mistake which is commonly committed by most of us to please the people around us because of our emotion and love for them or may also be due to societal pressure. We need to understand that if someone truly loves us, then our happiness would be their prime importance. They would never pressurize us to adjust to a situation which is not morally right or makes us unhappy. We need to get out of our illusion and gather the courage to take the right decision. Those who truly love us will not only understand our situation but will also appreciate our courage and right decision with time.

CHAPTER 13

My phone screen was flashing with an unknown number which seemed to be an ISD call. I picked up the call. A girl's voice on other side speaking in American accent surprised me. The voice seemed familiar to me, but I was not sure about it as her English was really confusing me. Finally, Amita started laughing. She successfully fooled me.

"Oh my God, Amita, I am going to kill you. You have called me now. Last time you called you were an Indian, you know?" I said in an annoyed tone.

After going to Canada, Amita had called me only thrice. Though we were in touch online but I missed talking to her with ease. We used to live next to each other for three easy years and now she calls thrice in two years.

"Yaar, I thought that you should also get to know how people talk here." Amita said teasingly.

I laughed "I know... I know your generous nature."

"I have someone here with me who wants to talk to you." Amita said handing over the phone to someone.

"Hello, Aarohi." It was Ravneet. I heard her voice after so long and felt very happy.

"Wow, Ravneet, such a pleasant surprise. You two are together. It must be fun." Now I was missing them even more wishing I could be there with them as well.

"Yes, we are having fun. Amita has learnt to cook and is cooking for me. Cool, naa? We meet sometimes on weekends. But we always miss you, babes. We thought of calling you up this time." Ravneet told.

"It feels so good to talk to both of you together. I, however, should kill you both for not calling me earlier. But I am so happy now, so maybe tomorrow." I laughed as well as both of them. "You people are lucky to be together. You know how much I miss you, guys?""

ISD calling isn't a cheap affair especially for students and therefore we kept it short, but the phone call kept echoing in my mind for a long time. I was thinking about my life without my dear friends and was mentally absent from my work. I knew I was not going to get back those golden carefree hostel days.

I could not concentrate in experiments that day and decided to spend my day writing research paper for the science journal based on my work done so far. Many of my new findings were good and were suggesting towards a great research in the coming future.

I was busy in my thoughts of Amita and Ravneet mixed with the thoughts of hostel and a little about the paper too when Nidhi walked in. She looked quite panicked in the lab. She went to the window of the lab and stood there. I was engrossed in my work so did not notice her at first. Then I heard Nidhi sobbing. I was surprised hearing her cry and went to her.

"Everything okay with you? Why are you crying?" I asked hesitantly. I was not sure how Nidhi was going to react.

"All my hard work is wasted, Aarohi. I do not know what to do now." Nidhi replied weeping.

"If you don't mind, tell me, but please stop weeping. Tell me exactly what happened? May be I can help." I asked genuinely concerned.

"I had kept the sample materials for rest of experiments in the refrigerator as they need to be preserved in low temperature, but the sweeper switched off the refrigerator by mistake in the evening yesterday. Today, when I went to collect the sample, it was already too late and the sample is spoiled. Now, how will I complete my work? New sample will need another two months to arrive. All my efforts will be wasted if I have to wait till then." Nidhi started weeping again.

I knew how bad it feels if all the efforts are wasted, especially by someone else's fault. I felt bad for Nidhi. Nidhi has always been so rude to me. From day one she never appreciated me. I could easily help Nidhi, as we both were using similar samples and reagents, but I couldn't get over her behavior in the past. I was just about to leave her alone when I remembered what naani told me the last time we met. 'Sometimes, Aarohi, it's difficult to be good to someone, but don't let it stop you from helping others.' As the moment flashed in front of my eyes, I decided to help Nidhi.

"If you won't mind, I can help you. You probably know we use same reagents and sample. You are welcome to use them while I order for new ones, and you can reimburse them to me."

Nidhi knew I could help her, but she also knew what she had been doing to me. She knew she never helped me, not even for menial things. That was why she was hesitant to ask for the help herself.

"Aarohi, thank you. I need some sample material. If you can share some of the sample you have with me, my work would be completed. I will pay you the cost that you would incur and I have ordered it so I will ensure that it reaches soon. You are being a huge help to me. You didn't have to do it, but you are. Thank you so much."

"You can use the sample. I do not need all of it now. I will use the one you order, once it comes."

Nidhi was finally happy hearing this and did not know

what to say. I could see happiness and repentance in her eyes, but the second thing that I learnt was not to expect anything in return. So I left without asking anything else from her.

With my help Nidhi carried her work on time. Her attitude towards me had also changed. She tried to help me wherever she could and praised me in front of others which would bring a smile on my face.

Nidhi submitted her thesis on time and soon her time to leave came. She called me in a corner of lab on her last working day in the department.

"I am sorry, Aarohi. I did not help you when I could, but you were always nice to me. On the top of it, you have played such a big role in completion of my work. I will always remember your favor and cannot be thankful enough for this." Nidhi said bidding goodbye to me.

I never expected an apology from Nidhi. So, I was surprised when I got one. "It was my pleasure to be able to help you." I said smiling. Nidhi hugged me and left.

'I was so worried and clueless about dealing with the problem I was facing, but I did not know that the solution was so simple. Just to be who I am. Just to keep on doing good and not letting the evil nature of others affect me. Thank you, naani, for this valuable advice which is going to help me all my life.' I thought relieved. I realized that when I expected less and did my deeds without expectations, I felt at ease in my heart.

DEEDS

Evil cannot be defeated with evil. Hatred cannot be lessened with hatred. It's the love which cuts the hatred and evil. Your deeds play an important role in determining your personality. You can act clever and try to fool others but it all reflects in your personality. You cannot hide your personality for a long time. Most importantly evil done to others surely comes back to you in one form or the other.

People visit temples, churches, mosques etc. to pray every day while some take out time from their busy schedules to worship their God at home. They think that doing so would help them please God and open the doors of heaven for them, but at the same time when they return to the real world after worshiping, they are proud and mean to people and treat the poor badly. All their efforts to please god, visits to temples and hours spent worshiping dissolve there and then. Such people can never please god.

Only good deeds done selflessly with a pure heart is the way to please God and bring peace to your soul. When we succeed in pacifying our soul we succeed in pleasing God because God resides within every one of us. Helping people in need, understanding other's situations, donations and charity for the poor without expecting anything in return is the pathway to your happy soul.

Many times, our deeds and our duty involve some sacrifices from us. 'Sacrifice' sounds like a heavy word having a deep meaning. We mostly do sacrifices for the people we love. It mainly revolves around ensuring the happiness or wellbeing of those we care about. Sacrifices are an essential part of our lives. It may be a big sacrifice or a small one but they are essential for our lives. A sacrifice which is big for someone may seem too small to the other person. However, it does not demean or devalue its importance. A sacrifice helps us understand that someone else's happiness is of more importance to us than our own.

We all sacrifice something in different phases of our life. A woman sacrifices her own needs for her family, a father sacrifices his own dreams for fulfilling dreams of his kids, a soldier sacrifices his family life and most importantly his own life for his country, lovers make big and small sacrifices to be with each other. Life is based on these sacrifices which further contribute to our deeds.

Many a times, we regret for the sacrifices we made in our past. We do not have to regret as all those sacrifices, all our decisions have brought us where we are. While we make sacrifice, there would be someone who would also have sacrificed for us directly or indirectly. The whole world sustains because of these sacrifices. Never regret a sacrifice you did because it was the right thing for you to do at time. Love with an open heart, accept life as it comes, and embrace happiness even if it comes with some sacrifices because it is all worth it at the end.

CHAPTER 14

I was running in a desert and was very thirsty. I was finding it very hard to move my feet and run anymore. I looked around and saw that I had reached at the top of a sand dune. I could see the desert around me. Everything seemed so small from the top. I again looked for water, but could not find it. I was lost, alone and thirsty. It was getting dark and my anxiety was also increasing with the increasing darkness. I felt panicked and woke up with a start. I still felt burning in my throat for I was thirsty in real. Still trembling with the dream I looked around on the side table and found the glass of water. There was water.

It, again, was an early morning dream. I checked my mobile phone for messages and got one. It was from the science journal people who wanted to publish my second research work in their journal. It said that my work has been accepted for publishing and I could check the details on my email id.

My eyes bulged and got wide open. All the morning laziness was gone. I opened the laptop and checked email. My happiness knew no bounds. Happily, I went for my morning walk. I could feel the beauty of nature around me. Everything seemed positive. I sat on a bench and looked around. My mind was at peace today. The dream felt like a faraway lost land.

I closed my eyes so that I could feel the nature to its best. I could hear the birds chirping; feel the wind strokes in hair, its soothing touch on my cheeks and the peaceful environment around me. I loved the feel of nature and it was bringing a lot of solace with it. Slowly, I went into deep trance where I could hear nothing just the sound of my breathing.

I could hear my heart beating loud and clear and then I experienced something very unique and liberating. I was not able to listen to anything; there was just a wonderful feeling of liberation and freedom. My mind was free as if it was outside my body. I had never felt like this before. Then suddenly, I was back to my conscious mind as if I had been woken up from a dream. I opened my eyes and glanced at the watch. It had been half an hour since I was sitting there; unaware of the surroundings I was sitting in. Hurriedly, I headed back towards the hostel to start my day.

'What did I experience today in the morning?' I was thinking sitting in the lab; it was such a unique experience. 'I have been feeling so peaceful since then as if some storm inside me has ended. I am so much at peace after this experience.'

"What are you thinking, Aarohi?" Ankit asked.

"Nothing," I replied. "Just about the work, and usual."

Ankit had always been friendly with me. By now, I had become pretty acquainted with his nature. We became kind of friends too. Though it was not exactly friendship but it was better than my relationship with my other seniors whose faces always seemed like they were being taken for a kidney transplant.

However, I did not tell Ankit anything about the dream, thinking that he would not understand it and may even mock me for the dream.

"You are so lost and anxious these days. I think you should try meditation." Ankit said.

"Meditation?" I asked surprised. I did not expect such

spiritual term from an easy going person like Ankit.

"Yes. Meditation is a great tool to pacify your soul." Ankit replied seriously.

"What do you know about it?" I asked.

"Well I know a lot of things. You can ask your doubts if you have any." Ankit asked in a matter-of-fact tone.

I felt guilty for being judgmental towards him and considered telling him about my morning's experience. 'May be he can tell me why I feel so peaceful.' I thought.

I told him in detail and asked "I am feeling so peaceful after that, but I do not know how it happened?" I said. "Was I meditating, by chance?"

"Kind of. It's simple, Aarohi. You were nearest to your own soul at that moment. You spent time with yourself. You felt what is inside you and it's obvious to bring peace to you. This is just like meditation, but for a better understanding you will need practice. You should practice it regularly and you will feel the change in your personality, perception and even things around you will mean different for you, everything. *When your words are heard but not understood, when you breathe but are not living, when there is silence but you are not at peace. Meditate and find everything within you.* Sometimes, meditation is the best medication for your soul."

I was astonished to hear such spiritual words from Ankit. I had definitely judged him wrong. He was much more than what he appeared to be. I was happy to have him as a friend.

"I never expected to hear such wise words from you, Ankit." I said.

"Aarohi, you are lucky to join as a research scholar under Mr. Ojha, but you are the luckiest to have met a genius person." Ankit pointed to himself and started laughing.

I too started laughing with him. Suddenly, I felt it was so

easy to be friends with Ankit, who always was there, instead of others who didn't even bother talking in proper way.

"Ankit, I am sorry."

"For what?" He looked panicked.

"I didn't take out time to properly talk to you. I might have even avoided you sometimes."

"Hey. I too had things to deal. It's okay. We can be good friends now. Everything has a time, Aarohi. This is for our friendship." He extended his hand out. "Friends?"

I shook hands with him and nodded. 'May be, he was just like this always. I just didn't bother to look closely. I have been very judgmental about him. I should not be judgmental about people. They might really be good deep within their heart.'

JUDGEMENTS

We see people judging each other every day on various personal and societal parameters from being good parents, good wife/husband, choice of clothes, timings of going out to working till late hours. We often crib about people judging us for something we may have done with a different attitude, but we never notice, how much judgmental we, ourselves, can be without even noticing it. We start to judge people without considering their thinking and attitude. There are so many other factors that are to be considered before making an opinion on someone, but we forget considering them, taking an easy way out by assuming things. We try to see things from our own lens, our own understanding, our own mindset and the things which do not fit in; we judge them.

We need to understand that we live in a world with different people who have different personalities, different choices and different problems in life. Why do we judge them? Who are we to judge them? Why cannot we be more acceptable, more open minded and more generous to others?

Humans lag behind in the quality of lending a helping hand rather than being judgmental and pulling other's leg. There are many people who find satisfaction and happiness in other's loss.

Instead of being judgmental towards each other and assuming other's choice as unacceptable, we need to be open in our thoughts and be more acceptable towards people's independence, to let them live their lives as they want. Being different from each other is the beauty of life. It adds to colors and variety in our life and makes it worth living.

CHAPTER 15

I started practicing meditation regularly. The more I was doing it, the more I was getting closer to myself. I was feeling more positive, developed more patience and was finding the world more beautiful. Negative things were not affecting me as they did earlier. The radiance was reflecting on my face as well as work.

"Hey. Wassup?" Ankit said entering the lab and keeping his bag at the side table.

"All good." I said engrossed in the work. I was trying to look for some specific cells with one eye focused on the microscopic view of those dangerous cells which were causing deadly disease of cancer in my experimental sample.

"You are prospering at work. Good going." He said coming towards me.

I looked up at him and smiled.

"Do you mind having a cup of tea in the canteen? The chef cooks awesome noodles these days. We can have that too." He said.

"Not today. May be some other time." I replied casually getting back to the microscopic view of the life threatening cells.

"Oh come on. It won't take much time. You look puzzled and stressed out. I think you need a tea break. Trust me it won't be a long one." He said.

"Hmmm... Okay. May be you are right. Let's go." I said

taking off surgical gloves from my hands and we left for the canteen.

We grabbed the chairs as we sat on the opposite sides of the table in the canteen and ordered noodles and two teas.

"So, Miss Aarohi, how are you feeling? Two of your research papers have been published and you had achieved some astonishing results on breast cancer. You must be on cloud nine now?" He joked.

"Nothing like that. It's just that I am in a calm place in my mind. Sometimes I wonder if anybody up there is taking care of me specially. I think my naani and God are taking care of me." I said smiling at him.

"They surely are, but that happiness should reflect on your face too. Isn't it?" He said taking a sip of the hot tea. Tea and noodles were served on the table.

"Still there is some time to rejoice. Actually, I am now stuck at a point in carrying forward the experiments and not getting the desired results. Though I am reading a lot of books and even searching it online to get more knowledge about this to get an overview of the issue from different angles, but still it is not entirely helpful."

"Why don't you inform Mr. Ojha about it? He has a lot of experience in the research that you are doing. I think he can guide you through it. He has also helped me so many times in such situations. I tell you, he is a genius. His guidance always helps me." Ankit said as I kept nodding to his suggestion. I too felt that I should take Mr. Ojha's help at this crucial point of my research.

"I think you are right. I will go to meet him after this tea break." I said as I smiled thankfully at Ankit.

"See. I told you that you needed a tea break to clear your mind. I am also no less than a genius." Ankit joked with a self-praising tone.

"Yes. Though I did not want to agree with you on this,

but now I have to. You are a genius." I said smiling.

I went straight to Mr. Ojha's room with my research findings to discuss the problem that I was now facing at work. Mr. Ojha listened to the issue carefully and went through my research findings.

"Aarohi, I think you are doing a very basic mistake at the start of the process. I feel you should decrease the speed at which you are carrying out the centrifugation process. I may help to separate the cells properly. Just try that." Mr. Ojha suggested.

Finally, my hard-work yielded fruits and I found the key to the lock. Mr. Ojha's suggestion worked liked a miracle. I finally got the results which no one had expected. I went to Mr. Ojha and told him about the experimental results. Mr. Ojha was happy to know about it. He came with me to the lab to check the results. He was happy because he understood the importance of the work that I had done and its relevance for the mankind.

"You have done a marvelous work. This should be the happiest day of your life as a researcher. I have been seeing you work so hard, Aarohi. I am proud of you." He said appreciating my work. "For a scientist, nothing is more rewarding than his efforts bearing fruits and getting positive results. I have been thinking to recommend you to be sent to the Conference of Scientists and Researchers which is to be held in London. You can present your work there on behalf of our university." Mr. Ojha genuinely appreciated my work that day and addressed all my seniors about it.

"Oh my God! Thank you so much, Sir. I am so overwhelmed to know this." I replied happily.

Mr. Ojha had not felt anyone's work to be presented at international platform in recent years. This was an immensely important honor and opportunity that I was presented with. I wanted to work really hard for it and achieve so much in life.

After a week, I submitted my passport and other documents for completion of Visa formalities and I was really happy about the whole thing.

"We should never leave hope. I am thankful to God for giving me the patience. It was good that I maintained my trust in my guide. Everything comes to you at the right time. You need to maintain your patience and trust. Losing trust in people sometimes increases your hardships in life." I was feeling delighted and was thankful to Mr. Ojha.

I was on seventh heaven and had no way of expressing my gratitude towards life. Each and every time in my life I felt this way, I thanked people around me. That's what I did. I thanked everyone around me for their presence and help in life.

GRATITUDE

Life gives us so much to be happy about that we should never fail to express our gratitude for it. When we thank someone for the things happening in our life, when we give due credit to where it lies, we help them in feeling good about them. In return they feel good about us too. Helping others is a good nature, and to keep it maintained, a person expects nothing but a little appreciation for the efforts.

If we do that, it makes us humble and lifts our character. It shows us the importance of others in our life. But most importantly, it also keeps us grounded. It helps us understand that the victory that we got has devotion of a lot of people to it. People who have importance in our lives, may or may not be actively participating in it, but always share a piece of victories and commend us for them. Sharing our victories gives a sense of togetherness with people.

We should understand that only the person who keeps his friends close to him and works with his team, giving them due credit in his life, can feel the happiness of achievement in true sense.

Meeting Aditya made me to go back to the nostalgic memories of the bond I shared with Rudra. All these years, I had not met anyone with whom I felt like meeting again.

With the experiences of life, I had learnt to be practical. Once heart-broken, I had stopped to give full mind and heart into a relationship because of the pain and heart-ache I suffered previously. I feared to go through suffering and agony again. *The sharp ache felt long back fades away, but tenderness in the heart always remains*. So, I had convinced myself to shut the doors of my heart as I thought that the emotion of love was no longer my cup of tea.

Coming out of my thoughts, I reminded myself that I was in London, on my first foreign travel. The outside world seemed beautiful. *As the views outside changed, I wondered, whether my life was moving faster or my car.* I had watched all the Harry potter movies more than once and was excited to be in London. A neat and clean, beautiful city with cute houses and picket fences, that were very different and beautiful. I was enjoying the feel of my second dream being fulfilled. My dream of travelling the world had finally commenced.

CHAPTER 17

I was being taken somewhere by my parents. The place seemed to be lonely. I was wondering as to what was happening. But I could feel that I was not well. There was something wrong with me as I felt frail.

Suddenly, I felt my soul leaving my body. In no time, it was outside my body and was as light as air. My body was numb. I was in a room in some distant area and there were other souls too inside that room who were trying to take my soul with them. My soul wanted to go back to my body and was struggling to be heard by my parents. I looked at my parents who still had my hand in theirs. I felt a need to connect with them, to tell them that I want to come back. Suddenly, I woke up panting from this nightmare. I had seen a strange dream again and was feeling a mild headache. I could not sleep further. I felt a little distracted from my surrounding, but a vague memory of being in London was still alive in my head; getting down at Heathrow Airport, talking to a nice stranger. I decided to see around in London and threw off my blanket.

"I have had so many weird dreams and most of the time they were just dreams, but all the time they have been followed with some kind of life events. *May be my heart voices its notion through dreams and I wake up every time to shrug it off.*" In the buffet hall, while having the breakfast, my thoughts were still lingering around my dream.

"Through this dream I had a deep realization that

everyone is alone in this world. We all come to this world to play our respective roles, but in the end, we are all alone. All these relationships are temporary. Only our soul is permanent." I thought and smiled to myself.

I looked around and saw people moving in the hall. I realized that I was amongst the people who may be very rich in monetary terms but also rich in terms of knowledge. "But the very first attribute, reflected by one's personality to anyone who meets him the first time is the generosity and humbleness, which attracts people."

"Hi." I was still lost in my thoughts when I saw a guy waving towards me.

He was coming towards my table with his breakfast plate in his hand. I was trying to place him whether I knew him or not when he said, "Hi. I am Rishabh."

Oh yes, I knew him and had talked to him regarding work over phone many times, but it was the first time I was meeting him in person.

"Yes. Of course, Rishabh. Hello. It's nice to finally meet you."

"Same here, Aarohi."

"I saw your presentation. It was very nice"

"I was really amazed to see your research work too. It's really impressive."

"Thank you so much"

Rishabh was an Indian working in US. He had also done his initial research work under Mr. Ojha and then moved out of India afterwards. He too had come to present his work and inferences in the conference.

"How is Mr. Ojha?" he asked.

"He is good."

"Is he still engrossed with work so much like he used to do back then?" Rishabh asked in a joking tone.

"Yes, pretty much. I can safely say...even more." I laughed heartily. "But if you remember he manages his time very well."

"Yeah you are right." He laughed too. "Okay. Apart from work, did you get time to see around?"

"Not yet. But I am going out today to see all the places in this beautiful city, I have arranged for a tourist guide too and the London tour bus. I heard that's really fun."

"That is great. I am also free till evening and had similar plans. Can I join you?" he asked politely.

"Yes sure. The more the merrier." I smiled. I really didn't want to roam around alone. Such a beautiful city and I didn't have a friend to share all this with. Rishabh wasn't actually a friend, but an acquaintance was better than being alone. Mom had gifted me a new selfie stick, but still I did not want to take all selfies alone. Now I could have someone to tag along.

"I have made a list of the places to visit. I had done a bit of research on tourist places before coming here" I said delighted.

"That's cool. You have taken off my load then. I hate planning a tour, but now I have my tour planned already. All thanks to you." He said laughing. I too smiled.

"The tourist guide is waiting outside. Let's get going." I said finishing the last bite of the sausage sandwich.

CHAPTER 18

"Aarohi, you remember the poem "London Bridge Is Falling Down" that we used to recite in nursery rhymes." Rishabh asked. We were standing on the famous London Bridge.

"Yes, I remember." I replied as the nursery rhyme rang in my head. Those childhood memories where me and my friends held each other's hands and sang nursery rhymes, dancing and jumping in a circle. "Also, whenever I saw any movie sequence shot here, I always wondered how it would feel to be here in reality." I replied with a tone of elation in my voice. "But let's not get the London Bridge falling down just yet; I am really anticipating to visit other places too."

He laughed hard. He was amiable and easy-going. I was glad he tagged along.

After spending some time at the London Bridge and clicking some pictures, we headed towards Westminster Abbey, Big Ben and Trafalgar Square. I felt so proud to see the statue of Mahatma Gandhi in the Parliament square of London.

"See, he was such a great leader that he has inspired whole of the world including the Britishers, against whom he fought for freedom of our nation." I was proud.

"Yes. He was one such person who has inspired the whole world, Aarohi. Not only here, but in US too people idolize him. He is my favorite too."

Madame Tussauds Museum also had wax statues

of many Indians. I got pictures clicked with my favorite celebrities and was too exhilarated.

As our city tour moved forward we reached the Buckingham Palace which is residence and administrative headquarters of the Queen Elizabeth. I clicked photo with the Palace guard, who of course never even managed a smile.

"Becoming successful in life may mean to earn money for majority of people. The people living in Buckingham palace have such huge amount of money, but are they the happiest in the world?" I asked Rishabh.

"Aarohi, our mind has been conditioned so well about the importance of money and the concept of being poor. While in actual sense, there are many people who have copious money, but are still penurious because they are not wealthy at heart. *A rich person is the one who is evolved as a human being with virtues of helping, generous nature.* It brings true happiness to a person." Rishabh said it so easily.

I liked his easy manner. I felt that I was roaming around with a friend. I also had seen instances where people shared whatever little they had because they understood the pain of being needy.

"The people who earn with their hard work realize the worth of these emotions. You may have little money but a big heart. If you have a big heart, spiritual mind and are clear about your goals in life, you are a much richer person than you think."

"You think quite deeply for a person so young. If I hadn't known better, I'd have thought you were a writer." He smiled.

"Yes, I do. Not always but many times." I replied smiling too. "I hope I am not boring you."

"No. Not at all. I am just trying to find a place to run away." He laughed at his own jest. "Not many people have such deep and intelligent mind."

"I know. I am so intelligent." I replied smiling. The

"Change of Guards" ceremony had started and we both got busy watching it and capturing the moments in our camera.

Rishabh had to leave the tour early due to his prior assignments. I bid him Good Bye and went ahead alone.

"We would now proceed towards our last place to visit ... "The London Eye" said the tour guide. London Eye, the giant Ferris wheel on the banks of river Thames. It was evening but still the sun was shining. Thanks to long days in Europe in summers. The Day and Night cycle was very different from India and was a different experience for me. It was 8 at night and the sun had not set.

Gentle gale was grazing my cheeks as if it was also happy with me and was giving me a peck. I felt amazing as I proceeded towards the top of the wheel. I was travelling to the top slowly just like I was prospering in my life. The view of this beautiful city was breath-taking. I could not decide which area of the city was more beautiful. River Thames was the highlight and added to the mesmerizing views. I could see most of the places I had visited in the City Tour when the views changed from time to time. I wanted to stop the time and re-live this moment again and again.

The giant wheel had now started proceeding downwards. I thought of the cycle of life which was just like the giant wheel. *Anything that reaches the top has to follow a downward trend too one day.* It is tough to be successful but tougher to maintain the same level of success. It is the rule of life that nothing is permanent. "We should always remember our roots, identify our real-self and be humble in all situations in life." I thought.

EMOTIONS

The purpose of our life is to be free. The freedom to freely express, to do what we want to do without being too much worried about the present and future, to release our soul of the boundaries created in our minds. The basic human nature is open and liberal which we try to change as we grow up.

By doing this, we only hinder our own development and prohibit ourselves from experiencing the beautiful world which is full of different people, emotions and experiences. Just like a soldier is meant to fight, a sword is meant to kill, we are born to live and experience life.

We can never master our emotions, but we can let ourselves be free, to feel every emotion as intensely as we can. The irony of today's world is that freely expressing your emotions is considered a taboo. When we are born, we are free souls, we express exactly what we fell, we don't think twice before crying, laughing or showing delight and pain, but as we start growing up, we start learning to conceal our feelings. From childhood itself, parents encourage their kids to repress their feelings. The parenting dialogues like "You are a strong girl, you should not weep" or "Boys are brave, they don't cry" are such examples. We teach the kids inadvertently from the very beginning that being emotional is a bad trait and should not be exhibited. The kids are taught that being strong means to quash your emotional side.

They implement such teachings in every aspect of their life. They try to suppress what they feel and succumb at expressing emotions like anger, love, sadness. This is the basic cause of increasing cases of stress, anxiety and depression at a young age. We put so much unnecessary strain on our minds that we end up affecting our health. Being emotional is not a negative trait. It is the freedom to express what you feel as a human being.

A step further, if you are empathetic enough to

understand other's emotions and emotional state, then you are exceptional. Being empathetic is not everyone's trait; you are blessed if you are endowed with it.

All we need to do is to get rid of the unnecessary boundaries created by us in our own mind because they limit our capabilities and freedom to feel our emotions and live life to the fullest. Life is limitless and once we learn to be free from the boundaries in our mind, we realize our full potential and we grow with a free mind and free soul.

CHAPTER 19

I enjoyed my stay in London. Everything from presentation to London city tour went better than as planned. It was a dream came true for me. I made new friends and met the dignitaries in the field whose research papers and journals I had been reading and getting know-how. They had come from all corners of the world.

Reaching back to India, I went home. I had been missing home, throughout my trip, especially Aakriti who had told me to bring a list of so many things from abroad. I thought it would have been nice if Aakriti was also there with me in the trip. We both shared beautiful bond of love and friendship. Though I was elder to Aakriti, but we were more of friends than siblings. I would be flabbergasted with her wisdom and clarity of thoughts mostly. I would take her advice many times when I was in a dilemma.

"Have you heard this song?" Aakriti asked turning on the volume of the car's speakers. "It's a Himachali song. I do not fully understand the lyrics but I am in love with its music."

I also loved music, but my taste of songs was very different from Aakriti. When we were young we used to quarrel for the songs to be played in the car, but now I also loved the songs Aakriti played because that reflected her love and sense of sharing her interest with me.

I was listening to the lyrics carefully and understood most of it except a few words. We were out on a long drive.

"How was your London trip?" Aakriti asked.

"It was superb. You know, initially I was nervous about meeting and interacting with people with such high intellect, representing my country in front of people from different countries who spoke different languages. Gradually, I realized that people may live in different countries, may have different languages, different dialects, but the inner make up of a human being is same everywhere. Humans understand the language of humanity and love, the wonderful language of gestures and body language which is more or less same for everyone. Also, a look into the eyes of a person is enough to reflect his personality and intensions."

"Yes, you are right. It means it was a good exposure for you." She said.

"Yes, a good exposure for work and also a wonderful glimpse of this beautiful city." I replied.

Aakriti stopped the car on the roadside and asked me to follow her. We started rambling up a hill together, on the road side.

"Where are we going?"

"I have searched a beautiful place for us to sit and relax. It's just at a little stretch. Keep walking."

I loved Aakriti's venturesome nature. While Aakriti sometimes became more careless to her safety, I always remained to the safer side of life. We have been different and I understood that, but I was her elder sister, which made it obvious of me to be worried for her.

We had reached the top of this small rocky hill. I was enthralled to see the view from there. It was so fascinating. Surrounded by mountains, river was flowing towards a side and the sun was ready to set. It was one of the most beautiful views I ever shared with Aakriti. Though I had seen many such places, but she never accompanied me. We both sat there looking at the view.

"These days you are so busy, you do not even get time to attend my calls."

"Do not lie. I always make sure to call you back." I laughed.

"Hmm.. But do you get time to spend with the most important person in your life?"

"Who is it?"

"You, yourself sister." Aakriti was smiling. "You should take out time to spend with yourself, Aarohi. You look like you need time for yourself. You have gotten to a good pace in life, but you will regret later if you didn't give yourself some time. Alone Time is the most underrated concept for your mental health and your spiritual well-being." Aakriti took a serious tone, but looking at my face, she laughed. "Okay, I know I reversed the roles and am sounding more like you, but this is true. You don't want to sit in, alone, later and regret that you should have given time to yourself. May be find someone for you..."

I looked at Aakriti's face who dipped her voice at the end and kept looking at the last speck of sun visible on the horizon. When did she grow up so much?

"Aakriti.."

"Aarohi, I am just saying that you should just not be too occupied with work that someone crosses you by and you don't even know about it. I am not saying that you should tag a billboard about it." She laughed carelessly. It felt finally Aakriti was back.

"I know that whatever you are saying is right, but I am usually so much occupied with work that I rarely get time to do other things. You Know." I was feeling conscious, unlike her, but somewhere deep within, I knew, Aakriti was right at some level.

"All day long, we are engrossed with the materialistic

tasks and people who are small parts of life. We don't even look around us with that keen eye and sometimes miss most important things of life. The mind is occupied with so many things that we forget to know that the most important person in our life, we ourselves, has been neglected. People claim to understand each other while they fail to understand themselves." Now she was looking directly in my eyes.

"You are right; Aakriti, but I do not get likeminded friends there. My peer group is mostly of the people who are into studies so that affects my personality too."

"Why are you losing yourself in the process to fit into your peer group and societal norms? Whom are you trying to please by doing this? Aarohi, one should never feel sorry for being real and being what they really are. The more real you are, the more you are at peace. It boosts our mental health as there is no extra burden of pretending or to like what you actually don't like. I know Rudra's episode in your life has impacted you a lot. Though you do not mention it at all, but I know the impact it had on your life. You have surrounded yourself with work and colleagues and you are losing the person that you are apart from work." She said and paused.

"Aarohi, you are very special. You were not born to be like someone else or to fit into a group or be appropriate as per societal wishes. You were born to be you. You are unique. Feel like one. Give yourself some you-time. Liberate your heart. Let it breathe too. Everything will come. Eventually."

"I know whatever you are saying is right Aakriti, but it's easier to say and tough to implement as I have become so much habitual of this. Something changed in my life long time ago and I have grown accustomed to it. It will not change back."

"Never say never. Practice that self-love sister. Feel good about your real self. When you are real yourself, you start attracting the like-minded people where you can easily gel in. So, just be yourself, Aarohi."

Getting a philosophical lecture from Aakriti was new to me. Emotional, surprising, consciousness...so many emotions surfaced in my mind. I understood what Aakriti was trying to tell me.

"When did you grow so much?" I laughed and hugged my suddenly grown up sister.

"When you were busy trying to work against cancer, sister." Aakriti laughed back.

"Let's go back, it's getting dark. I promise I'll try my best."

I held Aakriti's hand in my hand and started walking back to the car. I was happy that my sister had grown so matured. She could handle life well, perhaps better than me.

SELF-LOVE

Love yourself without any guilt because Self-Love is the purest and toughest form of love. Feeling guilty about doing things which give us happiness is what we have been accustomed to do. Being guilty of enjoying the nature, when you could be doing the official work. Being guilty of leaving the kid home for work. Being guilty of not fulfilling the parents' dreams in order to pursue your dream.

Love yourself and your life guilt-free. It's your foremost responsibility to keep yourself happy, physically and mentally. We all have been conditioned to care for others, love others, sacrifice our own interests for our loved ones, but in addition to this self-love is also very important. In fact, it is the most important coz only a happy person can spread happiness.

Self-Love is not something instant; it's a journey that we travel to reach our destination of happiness. We need to learn to prioritize our happiness too along-with our other responsibilities. If we do not practice that, it would result in making a dull and stressed out individual out of us in long run.

It's just like the share-market where you will gain profit only when you know how to wisely invest; where to invest and how much to invest. If we invest our hundred percent in others and are left with no energy to invest in ourselves we lose our individuality and personality slowly.

It's very important to know about this investment of love and emotions and spare a part of love for yourself. Love yourself, do what you like, pamper yourself every now and then and you will see an improvement in your mental health. You will fell less stressed out, more happy and energetic.

Having someone with you, taking care of you and you letting him do it is a form of self-love too. Let people come close to you, to take care of you. It is a very happy feeling when you feel loved and taken care of by people around you.

You love yourself back for that.

Make space for your own priorities so that you are not drained out at the end of the day. Doing stuff that makes you happy is like charging your own batteries. It keeps you happy and charged and has long term benefits in today's busy life.

CHAPTER 20

I was back to the University campus. My life was back to routine. The work resumed its pace and I was back slumbering into research and paper writing with all the inferences that I got with my experiments.

After a particularly very exhausting day, I was in deep sleep. I dreamt that I was lost in a forest and Aakriti, who was back to being a 6-7 years old kid, was running with me. We were being chased by some men who had swords in their hand and wanted to kill us. I was now tired from running continuously, but was feeling the responsibility of saving Aakriti no matter what. Finally, we stopped under a canopy. I was breathless and was trying to catch hold of my breath when suddenly; a man appeared in front of us. I hid Aakriti behind me, but I did not know what to do now. How to escape from this situation? Then, out of nowhere, I got a sword in my hand and attacked the man. He screamed and started bleeding and I woke up startled. I could not sleep further. The rest of the night went restless with me waking up and sleeping off and on.

Aakriti's advice had affected me deeply. I was trying to have an overview of the way my life was going on. Work, food and sleep had become the major part of my routine. I had stopped singing, listening to music, playing table tennis and the things that I loved to do earlier. I had stopped meeting people, talking with my old friends and occasionally to myself. I realized that my life had become limited to my work and I haven't had one stimulating and interesting conversation, apart from Aditya Vardhan, in about ages.

I, now decided that I would take better care of myself; give myself more time and reasons to be happy. I decided the first thing I will do, will be to give time to my hobbies. I had made up my mind to prioritize the things that I loved to do. *All this time, I had been so engrossed in the background that I had forgotten to look at myself in the mirror.*

It was Sunday; I started my day at leisure. I switched on the radio, it was my favorite show. The theme of the show was to interview someone working exceptionally well in their respective field and the songs were played in between from time to time. In addition to the concept of the show, I loved the voice of RJ Manish.

"Friends it's raining outside and what does it remind you of. Well, it definitely reminds me of yummy pakodas with pudine ki chutney that my mom cooks for me. It used to be finger biting well." RJ Manish sounded enthusiastic. "However, our today's guest reminds me that pakodas are definitely not good for a healthy heart, but we can have it sometimes like in this rainy season. What say Dr. Aditya Vardhan?"

"Dr. Aditya Vardhan?" the name struck a chord in my mind as I remembered the familiar face of Dr. Vardhan and the conversation I shared with him on the airport exit. He said he was a doctor. "Can he be same?"

My mind was running fast as I turned up the volume.

"Yes, you can have it sometimes, Manish. In fact, you should do everything that makes you happy. That too is a part of heart health management. As a doctor, I too insist on taking care of heart through diet as well as through happiness. A stress-free heart is a healthy heart." Dr. Aditya said.

"You heard it from the expert folks. So grab that besan ka dabba and make some amazing pakodas this rainy season."

Manish was laughing again. "It is with these thoughts and intensions of helping needy that Dr. Aditya is organizing heart treatment camps in different parts of India where consultation and medicines will be given free of cost. He is well known for the work he is doing for humanity. The camp is soon to be organized in Chandigarh." RJ Manish said. Then he shared the website and phone number where more details regarding the medical camp were available. I ran for a pen. I wrote down the phone number quickly on my hand while Manish started a song about heart.

'Did I meet this person in London?' I thought excitedly. I opened the laptop and googled- 'Dr. Aditya Vardhan in Delhi'. I got a list of recommended sites. The first one had details of Dr. Aditya with his photograph and the exceptionally good work he was doing as a heart surgeon. I immediately recognized the picture as the man I met in London and was amazed.

'How pure by coincidence I met a guy so famous and so helping to others. He appeared so down to earth, as if a common man standing on airport while he was a medical celebrity equivalent. He surely has an amazing personality.' As my thoughts turned to Dr. Vardhan, I felt a sudden urge to talk to him. I had never felt like this in past so many years. I dialed up the number. It was the number of his hospital reception. I took Dr. Vardhan's phone number from the receptionist."

I had Dr. Aditya's number and my heart was racing fast. I was thinking if that would be awkward for me to call him. "What would he think of me? Would he even remember me? Would it be a good idea to call him?"

I was so confused, but I really wanted to talk to him and know him as a person. I finally thought to give it a shot and to call him.

"Hello." The good doctor picked up in two rings while I had half made up my mind to hang up.

"Hello. Is this Dr. Aditya speaking?"

"Yes"

"Uh... Hi. Ummm.. This is Aarohi this side."

"Hmmm. Aarohi? The London airport girl. Right?"

"Yes." I felt a sudden adrenaline rush running in my veins. I was happy that he remembered me. "Yes, the same."

"How are you, Aarohi?" He asked.

"I am good. Thank you, Dr. Vardhan. I was listening to a radio program and it appeared to be your interview. I heard about the...about the heart treatment drive you have started. I thought of... ummm... congratulating you for that." I was trying to find topic to talk about and the reason of calling him.

"Thank you so much. Where did you get my number from?" Aditya's smile was apparent from the phone and his voice.

"From your hospital's reception, Dr. Vardhan." I started to feel really embarrassed on the question. I had never done so much hard work to talk to a guy before and I had never called anybody so spontaneously.

"Aarohi, please call me Aditya. You know, I wanted to give you my number that very day itself... ummm... I had been thinking about you a few times." Aditya was stammering a bit himself, I noticed.

"Okay. I thought maybe you won't even remember me, given that we met for such a short time. Uh... Are you in Chandigarh? You were being interviewed on the show in Chandigarh." I asked curiously.

"Yes, but I am leaving tomorrow morning." Followed by a small pause was a question I could not explain why was I so happy at, but a tingle of electricity ran down my spine after hearing. "Ummm... Aarohi, would you like to meet me, in the evening? Only if you are free, I mean."

"Sure. I'd love to. I am free today in the evening." I was very surprised at my own reply. Nobody, not even Rudra, got such a response from me ever.

"Okay. Where can we meet?"

"Let's meet in Sector 17 Market. I already had planned to eat out today. So, we can dine there. There's an amazing restaurant that I have been to." Sector 17 was my favorite place to hang out in Chandigarh.

"Okay, then. See you in the evening. Bye." Aditya said disconnecting the call.

CHAPTER 21

I saw Aditya waiting for me from a distance. 'Pretty punctual. Busy and still punctual. Impressive.' I thought. Aditya looked dapper in a black shirt and blue jeans. I was a bit nervous. For the first time in life I was just following my heart.

"Hi" Aditya waved at me. He too seemed a bit nervous but was trying to hide it effortlessly. However, I could sense nervousness off him.

"Hi. Let's sit on this bench" I said moving towards the nearby bench under a tree in the market square. "It is my favorite place to sit. Whenever I come here, I sit here after my shopping. I like to observe people silently."

Aditya followed me to the bench and we sat there. When we started talking time flew. I told him about my life, my research, my motivations, my family, Aakriti, how I wasn't giving time to my life....

While I came to know that Aditya had faced more than his fair share of hardships in life. He had a failed relationship behind him which was a very bitter experience and then he never got married again. He was happy doing what he was achieving in his career and wanted to soar in his career for now. I had also wondered about his marital status because he seemed elder to me. I pretended to be sorry to know about the hardships he went through but somewhere inside I was also happy to know that my wish to know him more could be realized. I felt somewhere that my story was similar to him, just less formal ties.

May be that's why I resonated with his situation and could understand how hardships in relationships feel like. Like me, he too needed a friend, a companion with whom he could resonate and discuss things as he felt without being judged.

"I think we should get something to eat now. I am so much hungry." We both were so engrossed in talks that we had lost the sense of time.

"What are your views about marriage?" I asked ordering the food.

Aditya smiled. "See, it's easy to fall in love, but tough to maintain same level of importance and love for each other as time passes. It takes strong love bond, care for each other and small gestures which makes the other one feel wanted and appreciated. We need to settle for the person for whom our love bond is so strong that we are willing to do that extra effort to maintain the long-term relationship and vice versa. Else, we may end up being emotionally and mentally hurt.

"If you don't mind me asking, what happened that you had to face the harsh? You seem like a matured person, well sorted and all." Hesitation was ill-concealed in my voice. I was not sure of extent I was allowed to.

"Hmmm... Everything was wrong from the very first day. I could not find my companion and friend in my wife. Since, it was an arrange marriage, I did not know her earlier. You know, I was so busy with making my profession that I broke my life. I should have looked more closely before getting married, but at that time, everything was new and good. Slowly, the newness evaporated and the lack of compatibility surfaced. I won't say that we didn't try, we did. I tried a lot to find that spark and so did she, but sometimes companionship and marriage can be two very different things. Most of us try to look for both of them in the same person. I too tried to do that, but sometimes it becomes very difficult to perform well in both the roles since marriage comes with some responsibilities and adjustments. I do not blame her entirely for our failed marriage; we both weren't wrong, just looking from different places. The problem arises when we try to see the personality of our partner from our perspective of right and wrong. Then we expect them to change their habits or personality traits as per our liking. In my marriage, she did not understand me, my interests and I too finally gave up working on our sinking relationship." Aditya was looking into far away, or a time he left behind in his life. He sighed. "She must think the same. I never understood her and changed for what she wanted."

I felt like I probed his wounds again. His face had the signs of sadness I never wanted to induce. By thought of deflecting I suddenly uttered in a high pitch.

"The barbeque food here is nice. We should try that."

"Yeah, sure, Aarohi. You can order food of your choice. I love barbeque too." He smiled to me. I knew that he knew that I wanted to change the subject. I went through the menu and placed the order.

"Aarohi, you know, the key to any successful marriage or a relationship is acceptance? Having an open heart which accepts your partner as they are and giving equal importance to their liking and wishes. Since, we are life partners not siblings, we are ought to be different from each other and no one in this world is perfect. Hell, I and my brother are so different. How could my wife be same as me? The art of accepting our loved ones as they are is the basic need for survival of any healthy relationship. We just forget that sometimes." Aditya said, getting back to topic.

"People usually complain about the loss of the feeling of love as the relationship gets old. When the relationship is new we give each other the utmost importance and prioritize each other's likings and disliking, but as the relationship gets older, we start to take relationship for granted and it takes the back seat in comparison to our new priorities." He kept on talking his heart out while I just kept looking at his face, absorbing in the sadness and maturity shining out of his persona.

"I think that every event in our life has something good in store for us. We may realize it sooner or later so we should not be disappointed."

"Yes, definitely. I always wanted to be the best in my field of work. However, I tried but could not emerge as the best and was an average, but the struggle in my marriage helped me channelize my energy. Now, I am totally focused towards my work as I never was. I want to treat people, I want to help them. It brings me closer to my dream and also relieves me of the pain of loneliness. I have become closer to myself and have known myself better after this."

"To sum it all, all I'll say is that marriage is a bond which needs to be nurtured everyday like a newly planted sapling. Even the strongest feelings start to fade away if ignored for a prolonged time. Care, importance and standing together in tough phases of life strengthen the bond and keep lightening up the relationships. If you are capable enough to do that and are confident about your relationship of surviving these ups and downs, only then you should get into the marital bond."

I was surprised to see that Aditya could also speak so much in one go. Till now, I was the one doing most of the talking part and had assumed Aditya to be a silent person, but it felt great when I saw Aditya open up with me. It was start of our friendship which I had a feeling was going to be stronger with time.

RELATIONSHIPS

Freedom of soul is the most important thing in life. Sometimes we face such situations in life which force us to compromise on our freedom. There are some relations or people who are dear to us but they knowingly or unknowingly impact us in a way that we start compromising on freedom of our soul. Such things happen in the name of societal expectations mostly, but we must always remember that we should never lose ourselves, our personalities or the things that make us happy for sake of such relations.

Relations are not meant to force us to sacrifice our freedom to live as we want or do what we want to do. The relations that try to kill the freedom in us and try to tie us down as per their requirements are not real. In such cases, only one thing can survive either the relation or your personality.

There is nothing so important in life which is worth losing your own personality and freedom to and the people who try to curb others' real-self are themselves tamed by the society. They themselves are not free souls and do not understand the meaning of freedom. So, we should not commit the mistake of doing such unnecessary sacrifices for the sake of such relations. Those who truly love you accept you as you are and understand your likings and priorities. Those who don't understand are not worth your time.

Also, we should never raise other's expectations to the level that it becomes difficult to fulfill them. There are phases in life when we enter into new relationships in life. In our enthusiasm and happiness, we make promises and do things that we cannot fulfill later on. As it is said that we should never make promises when we are too happy. Same implies to the relationships.

We should always be grounded and do realistic things, things we know we are capable to do, things which we do not have to fake for the sake of making our relationship better. Such fake things and activities do not last long and when we land up in reality, it becomes troublesome for our relationship.

Always, do things which we can do with our whole heart for the rest of our life. Else, they become stressful and burdensome later on.

We all are different individuals and have to travel the journey of life individually. The results of our decisions have to be faced by us only. So, avoid being part of the crowd and do what you feel is good for you. This way you will either be happy or at least content that you tried your best to do what you really wanted.

CHAPTER 22

I was happy to have Aditya in my life. He was mature enough to understand me. Though I was not regularly in touch with him due to our different and busy schedules, but we talked whenever we felt to share something important.

I felt the bond that I shared with him could not be ordinary. It was the one that you share with your soulmate. Whenever I thought about him, I could feel the fireworks and celebrations going on inside my mind and soul as if it was some festival. I was happy that I had met my soulmate and wanted my life go on as it was destined.

I knew that Aditya did not have any plans to get married again, at least not soon, and I too had no such goals in recent future. It was a strong bond with him which I felt on the very first day, I met him, that made me pursue him to know more about him and make acquaintance with him. I could not myself explain the reason why exactly I was attracted to him, but I knew that it was certainly not because of some expectations of a sexual relationship or marriage. He seemed more like a family to me with whom I found the solace I looked for. I did not want to think of anything beyond that.

My soul connected with him in a way it had not connected with anyone else before. I wanted to listen to my heart and it was telling me to make Aditya a part of my life. It may be as a friend, an adviser, a lover; whatever, that did not matter. The nomenclature of the relationship was of least importance because I had realized that destiny had brought him in my life and everything was happening as destined.

Aditya was doing great in his work and he kept sharing his experiences with me. Through mails, calls or chats; whatever that our busy schedules would allow, we maintained our communication. I sometimes wondered how I never had time for anything else, but could accommodate Aditya in my life so easily.

I took advice from him in my research work anytime that I needed. Being from the medical field he would give me some valuable tips and knowledge.

It was my fourth year in Ph.D. and I was on my last parts of research and already had two patents in my name. As a result of my continuous efforts, I got selected among the 'Young Innovative Researchers in India' and was invited to present my research work in Paris.

"Aditya, it's amazing news but I am worried about the presentation. I have very little time to prepare for it. Also, my guide is not there to help me this time. I am seriously considering backing out of it. All the delegates and so many of my peers will be there. I can't mess it up. It'll be better if I don't present." I called up Aditya and shared this news with him.

"Aarohi, this is just the beginning of your success. You have to rise much higher in life. I can see you being successful and I know, you will achieve whatever you want in life. Don't back out. Work even harder if you have to, but you got to do this. This is a huge opportunity. Just relax and give it your best. Everything will go well."

"Learn to live in the present moment Aarohi. This moment will never come back. It is the moment of happiness, the moment when you got the news of your being selected to go to Paris. This moment once gone will be gone. *Be in the moment. Live in the moment. To relish flavors of life, nature and events around us, be mentally there, where you physically are.* It is the moment to celebrate, not to worry about future. Celebrate your happiness, celebrate your life. Keep all these worries for later."

"You are right Aditya. I am going to Paris, one of the most beautiful cities in the world. My desire to visit top of the Eiffel Tower is going to be fulfilled soon. I feel so blessed and happy."

"You should be happy Aarohi. Your destiny is unfolding itself slowly and is awarding you the deserved results of your hard work and right approach in life. You should feel yourself growing and should be happy about it."

"Yes Aditya, I can feel this growth not only professionally but also personally. The way my life is molding itself, I can also see the positive change in my attitude towards life and people."

"That is what I am trying to tell you. Live the present moment to the fullest and everything will fall in place in future too."

I smiled and felt proud of my friend who could make me feel alright when I felt chaotic inside. All my tension was gone. I wanted to celebrate this happiness and live the present moment to the fullest.

LIVE IN THE MOMENT

What can you trade off your happiness with? Most of us think that happiness cannot be traded off with anything in the world, but we ourselves trade off our day to day happiness with menial things and worries due to our mental absence from the present moment.

We have forgotten to live in the moment due to which we do not enjoy the happiness and beauty the present moment stores in it. The day to day worries make us absent minded. We are mentally absent from the present situations.

We may be sitting among our family or friends, but mentally we may be at our workplace. We may not enjoy the innocence of our kids coz we are engrossed with our mobile phones or gadgets. We may be sitting in mountains or a sea shore with all the natural beauty around us, but mentally we may be thinking about some different issues in life. The funniest part is that someday, taking care of other things, we might end up thinking about all that nature and beauty that we missed seeing at the right time.

We mostly do not allow ourselves to live the present moment to the fullest. The time we spend not living in the present moments, enjoying its beauty and peace is the time wasted. A collection of all such wasted moments is what makes a wasted life.

This habit in most of the individuals holds them back from enjoying the joys of life. Life is all about these small happy moments. Feeling the drops of rain on a swing, feeling the love of your loved ones, enjoying the music from your soul and letting the words you read in a book touch your mind and heart.

You can not possess the magical and beautiful moments of life. You cannot own the beautiful nature, the innocence of a baby, the calmness of river, the coldness of water. But you can live and feel them to the fullest when you are experiencing them.

Feeling everything to the fullest is an art which develops with practicing. It's also a kind of meditation and is directly linked to the concentration of a person. A person who practices it not only enjoys life in true sense, but also has a peaceful soul, strong memory and stress-free mind.

Just remember life is what is happening now. We never know what is stored in the future. So, value it, cherish it and love it in true sense.

CHAPTER 23

The day to leave for Paris had come and Aakriti was there to accompany me to the airport. She too had to catch her flight for Pune where she had recently joined at a new job. On our way to the airport, I saw a toddler running after a dog to catch it on the roadside.

"Hey Aakriti, look at that cute baby and the cutest little dog". I said. The toddler's mother was trying to stop her and the dog was also wagging its tail. The toddler fearlessly tried to catch hold of the dog. We loved that sight.

"This is such a cute view."Aakriti said excited.

'How can a baby be so fearless? Given a thought, as to from where this fear gets incorporated in our personality if we are born so fearless. May be as we grow up, we are taught to stay away from things which are dangerous, to be scared of them because of the harm they can cause to us. Just as the baby's mother is warning her for staying away from the dog. May be, we start learning from society and surroundings about the things we need to be afraid of and start behaving accordingly.' she added.

"Yes, you are right. I am also amazed at the fearlessness of that toddler." I said agreeing with Aakriti.

We had reached airport. I hugged Aakriti and bid her good-bye. She left for the ticket counter to board her flight, but the thought of the baby was still there in my mind. Sitting in the plane I was thinking about it. It reminded me of my childhood. My father is very fond of music and so am I. He wanted me to be a singer and used to teach me music and singing. He used to help me understand music, but I always had a stage fright so extreme. Whenever, I used to go on stage in front of audience, my hands and voice would tremble. I always tried to escape that experience, but dad made sure that he never missed a chance of my stage encounter. He used to get my name enrolled in every possible stage performance related to music.

At first, I hated this behavior, but with time, I realized that I was getting more comfortable on-stage and facing the audience. My voice now became more stable while singing and my hands stopped shaking. He taught me to face fears. He taught me to take control on my fears.

"Aarohi, fear in other words is the imagined story or situation, a lie we tell and convince ourselves with or an excuse we use to avoid the real situation. The basic element of fear is generally the Fear of unknown and unrevealed. *We are afraid of things which are unknown to us, the experiences we have never done. We are afraid of the surprises that we may get.* We feel that we may not be able to cope up with them, but once we learn to overcome it, we conquer our fears. You need to conquer your stage fear and that will only happen when you continue to do stage performances." He would say.

Today, I felt proud of having such an amazing father; a father who taught me to overcome fear which could have been ingrained in my conscious forever. Not only that, he taught me to be ready for every battle in life.

I was feeling thankful to my dad and thought of going home to meet him once I am back from Paris. Being busy with work, it had been 5 months I had not met him. He always tried to motivate me with his advice. Because of him I felt that I could take risks in life as he would be there with me. Fathers have their own way of showing affection to their kids whose importance we realize when we grow up.

He would tell "Everyone has some fears in life, the things we never want to happen to us. You may be scared to be left alone in a lonely place, a deserted road in a distant village, but if it actually happens, what choice are we left with. We have no choice but to face that situation. You may cry and call for help in the beginning, but then your mind starts to adjust to the situation. You start to understand that it's only by being strong and having faith in God; you can find the way out. *Its human nature that we do not learn to be strong till the time it's the only option that we have.* When you survive this dreadful night, you would not be the same person that you were the earlier night. Now, you would be stronger and more confident about pulling through such circumstances"

He would smile and say "I am not telling you to get into such a situation, but I want you to understand the essence of facing your fears through this example. If you would not have actually been in such situation, you would not have even thought that you can survive it. Similar, are the situations in life. Most of us fear to be left alone in life, fear to face a situation, the failure, to experience new things, to tell the truth, to be betrayed, to be heart-broken. The fear is to face the circumstances unknown to us."

"Ma'am would you like have something?" Air hostess's voice broke into my reverie.

I was on my seat in the plane and coffee was being served. I loved that frothy strong coffee. In fact, I had thought prior to boarding the flight that I was going to have coffee in the plane.

"A coffee please." I answered excited.

Enjoying my coffee, I was looking at the clouds from the window. The freedom of the clouds in the limitless sky reminded me of my limits, my boundaries. It was a 8 hours journey and I was enjoying it as it was my success journey too.

Few years back, I had never thought that I would be climbing the ladder of success this fast, but when you have hard work with luck and blessings on your side then there is no looking back.

DARKNESS

Running away from your fears in life is running away from yourself. Night is usually supposed to bring fear alongwith it. While Day and Night are part of life cycle, but the darkness of night generally symbolizes fear. All the negative thoughts are associated with darkness. However, if we think the other way, darkness symbolizes silence, peace, relaxation. In silence of night, you relive your memories, moments of solace soothe your heart, peaceful mind pacifies your soul and you fall in love with this intoxicating and addictive solitude. Hence, it's all about the viewpoint, whether we emphasize its beauty or its beast part. When you are afraid of the dark you may feel the beast in it. As you get acquainted with it, you fall in love with its peace and solace.

We may face situations in life where we really want to do something but the biggest fear we may face is the fear of being rejected by our loved ones. We may not be left alone physically, but there may be circumstances where we feel alone mentally, we may feel left alone even by nears and dears. We can only achieve things in life when we learn to overcome such phobias. The squalls in our life come for a purpose. If we survive them, we are not the same person that we were before we faced them. After all, the reason for such storms is to awaken us, to make us understand the beauty of life.

The crude truth of life is that evidently, we all have to live alone. The situations we come across in our lives have to be faced by us alone. We all play our individual roles in this life. So, we should not be afraid to be left alone or being rejected. The ones who are destined to be there with you will anyhow be with you in all conditions. By facing your fears and surviving these storms, you become aware of your strength, about your purpose in life, about the things that really matter to you.

Like the night is followed by a day. Darkness in life is

always followed by a bright day, but you need to be positive and believe in yourself. The wait period could be short or long, but it is always worth it. Being afraid of the dark means to be afraid of being yourself, being afraid to accept what you actually feel. The right things come to you at the right time. You just need to be patient and overcome your fears.

CHAPTER 24

"You are the next one for the presentation on stage" I was informed. I was in the auditorium to present my work in Paris. Though I was ready with my presentation, but was feeling nervous.

However, the presentation flew and glided. The applause I got after it was done was recorded in my mind. I was so euphoric after the presentation that I felt I might be flying for the rest of the program. The presentation went so well that everyone was impressed by the unique approach I had adopted in my work.

After the presentation, I along with other dignitaries was proceeding for lunch when a man approached me.

"Hello, Mam. My name is Philip Watson."

"Umm... Hello, Mr. Philip"

"Mam, our company is into manufacturing of medical instruments and we supply it throughout world. We think that the approach that you are using for the research is very unique and we would like to use a part of your methodology in our new microprocessors which will be used in Cancer related researches, medical centers and hospitals. We can discuss all the details of the association regarding it whenever you say. Only if you are interested, Mam." He said.

I was astonished to hear this. I never thought I would ever receive such an offer just after them hearing my presentation.

"It would be my pleasure if my work can be of any use to humanity. This is the sole purpose of my research. I would be fortunate to be able to contribute towards it." I suddenly felt I was so happy that I might start giggling right here, but I controlled myself.

I discussed the details with Philip and we exchanged our contact information, which he said was necessary as our association might go long. I was also informed about their company representative in India who would contact me on reaching India.

My Paris trip was more than successful. Apart from presenting my work at international level, I got the golden opportunity to directly contribute my services to the cancer patients throughout the world. I was feeling such a high in life. And to think I was about to drop out the opportunity because of my nervousness. I felt thankful to Aditya for encouraging me to come to Paris. I so much wished him to be there with me right now.

I always wanted to see Eiffel Tower and it was the best day to do that. I was already on the top of the world. So, I went to see Eiffel Tower and decided to spend my time exploring Paris with my team-mate Priyanka who was from India too and had also come to represent her research work. We both were staying in the adjacent rooms in the hotel and had become friends by now.

Soon, we both were on the top of Paris, top floor of Eiffel Tower and were enjoying the view of such a beautiful and well-planned city. I was enjoying my success and the view at the same time. I told Priyanka about my meeting with Phillip.

"There is a price for everything we achieve in life. Nothing is free in life. Just like in Mahabharata, while aiming at the fish's eye, Arjuna could only see the eye and nothing around it could distract him, you need to be that focused towards your goal in order to achieve it which is not an easy thing to do. I am sure we all have paid the price to reach to this level." She said.

I agreed to her views. "You are right Priyanka. When I was in hostel, I used to wonder, if my efforts were ever going to bear fruits or if I was just living an illusion through my dream. When you are young, there are lots of things which can distract you and make you doubt yourself. The college functions, hostel fun, late nights chatting and gossips with friends are of course bonus on that. It is very difficult to remain focused in life and be the odd one out when everyone else is enjoying. *When we are young it's 'odd one out', when we grow up it becomes 'standing apart from crowd'. It means the same, but the emotions behind them change.* It requires a lot of passion and determination towards your dream. We need a lot of trust in ourselves to be able to achieve it. When our soul craves to do something and we are clear that this is something that we want to achieve, that we are destined to do in life. Then we can do it only if we are ready to move mountains for it. Earlier, I used to think they are just words, powerful, but just words. However, my whole perception to them has changed."

Priyanka was looking at me with pride while I sank deep within my memories of my life and thought, 'Just like I paid the price of sacrificing the fun of hostel life. Spending most of the time in the library or in my laboratory was quite draining sometimes, but the goal I would achieve after this hard work kept me motivated and I happily paid the price for it. It may have been a very difficult time with lot of uncertainty, but the price I paid at that time makes me happy now and with time I realized that it was all worth it.'

"Yes, no hard work in the right direction goes waste. There is always a risk of failing and it all depends on you whether you take that risk or not. Whether you are confident about your instincts and hard work to achieve what you actually want." Priyanka's voice brought me back to the present. Priyanka was looking down at the clean blue waters of river Siene, but her voice conveyed that she was having some similar flashes of her life. Two people who never met earlier had similar goals in life. I was happy I wasn't alone.

I was back to India. My Ph.D. was almost on the verge of completion. I was completing the last series of experiments. Two new juniors had joined as research scholars under Mr. Ojha and I made sure to help them in every possible way I could. (I did not want them to face things that I did.) Excelling professionally and personally, I was paving my way towards my goal to be a successful scientist.

"Aarohi, Mr. Ojha has called you in his office." informed a research scholar while I was working with my paper.

I went to meet Mr. Ojha. I had not met him after coming back from Paris as he had also gone out. Sometimes, I felt really amazed by the amount of work he handled and the efficiency he had. Someday I would want to possess that level of efficiency.

"Good Morning, Sir." I said entering his office.

"Good Morning, Aarohi. Come have a seat."

"Everyone is appreciating about your presentation in Paris. I have my friends who had also attended the conference. They were all praising your work. I feel so proud and happy for you." His appreciation and pride was not at all concealed in his words. Most of times he spoke less, but today he spared no details of the proud moment that he got from his friends.

"Thank you, Sir." I was happy seeing him happy. After all he was my guide and has helped me so much.

"But the news I have for you supersedes everything." Mr. Ojha was smiling.

"What is it, Sir?" My curiosity made my eyes go wide.

"University Vice Chancellor had called me up this morning. He gave me good news regarding you. You have been selected by the Government of India among

Young Scientists to be presented with excellence award at Rashtrapati Bhawan."

"Oh my God!" The exclamation was the only thing I could manage out of my mouth. My ears could not believe what I had heard. It took me sometime to believe that it was actually happening. I had tears of happiness in my eyes. After recovering from the pleasant shock I thanked Mr. Ojha for his never-ending support and went to check the details sent to me by him on my email.

I couldn't sleep that night. I wanted to share the news with Aditya and was expecting the same excitement as my family and Amita, but he was out of country in New York for conference. I waited till I could catch him on call and talked throughout the night, revealing my plans of visiting Delhi soon. My excitement was on seventh cloud and my voice was revealing that well.

CHAPTER 25

Soon I had to leave for New Delhi. I was happy and feeling honored to receive such a prestigious award. I was a bit sad too as my parents and Aakriti had gone to Pune and would not be able to attend the award function, but at the same time, I was also excited due to the fact that I will be able to see Aditya after such a long time. I would be sharing my happiness directly to the person who was not just indirectly motivating and mentoring me, but was becoming a bigger and bigger part of my life.

I was packing my bag when I got a call from an unknown number. I thought of missing the call as my schedule was tight and I didn't want to be late, but then I picked up.

"Hello..." my voice was hurried.

"Hello, Aarohi."

The voice rang into my ears and I felt as if I was a statue for a moment there. The voice was so familiar to me that I could recognize it anywhere in the world. It was the voice that made my heart skip a beat always. A voice I hadn't heard for a very long time. A voice which still had the power of stopping me in my tracks. It was Rudra's voice.

I stood there with mobile phone in one hand and my unpacked toothbrush in another. I could not say anything. All memories flashed in my mind within seconds. My crying, his anger, his refusal, the scenes that I knitted, of his marriage, in my mind, everything.

"Hello Aarohi. Are you there?"

"Yes. Rudra. How are you?" I still did not comprehend well. "Umm... I am good."

"I am good too. Aarohi. I have called to congratulate you. I saw your name on TV in News today. I felt so happy and proud of you that I could not stop myself from calling you up."

"Thank You, Rudra. Your wishes are always special to me." I paused. I didn't know anything about him after that phone call. I cut all contacts with him. "I hope you too are doing well in life."

"Yes, Aarohi. I am, thank you."

"How's your...wife?"

"She is good. She sends her wishes too. I have become a father to a baby boy last month. His name is Ashu. It is a great feeling, Aarohi."

"That is great news. Wow. Congratulations, Rudra. I wish you and your family always stay blessed." I genuinely felt a tinge of happiness mixed with some other emotion I wasn't particularly aware of, but right now it didn't matter. "Rudra, I have to leave for Delhi today and I am in a bit of hurry, but I will definitely call you back some day."

"Sure, Aarohi. All the Best for the Award function." Rudra sounded... relieved... like the phone call was a pleasure mixed with pain for him too. He disconnected the call.

I sat on my bed trying to believe what just had happened. I had imagined getting a call from Rudra many times after my break up with him. I had waited so much for this one call that I didn't know when I stopped expecting it. Now, I got it when I was least expecting it.

Lost in my thoughts, I did not realize when I packed my bags and left for the airport. At airport, before boarding my flight, I felt like talking my heart out to someone. I could not think of anyone else but Aakriti. I picked up the phone and called her.

"Hello, sista."

"There was a time, Aakriti, when I kept looking at my phone with a hope to get a call or a message from Rudra. I used to sleep, holding my phone in my hand, as I feared missing his call due to my sleep. Now, finally when he has called me up, I am not feeling anything. No happiness, no excitement, nothing. I do not know what is happening?" I vented out my lack of feelings to her without any greeting or background. I knew she will understand very well.

"Aaru... You okay?" Aakriti became serious as I sounded very sentimental. "Yes, I am perfectly fine. I am just surprised at my own behavior and trying to understand my feelings."

"Aarohi, it is okay to feel this way. There is nothing wrong with you. In fact, it is absolutely right. Instead of being emotional or being overly excited by Rudra's call, you are feeling liberation, freedom from your own thoughts. You are finally realizing that your mind is freed from the feelings of heart-break and pain which you felt earlier even when you thought about him. It's a good sign, Aarohi. This is moving-on. This is what you wanted, a closure. Now you can finally close his chapter and throw it away."

"This is good? I was confused, thinking I might be in shock, but you are right. I am liberated. Finally Rudra has gone forever."

My flight was announced. "Thank you, Aakriti. I feel better. Now my flight is announced. I will call you later."

"Fly well. Not just the flight, but your life too."

I disconnected the call hurriedly and moved towards the queue for boarding the flight. 'I couldn't talk to him much, but my heart somehow feels lighter now. This phone call was so important to make me realize that I have been liberated and detached from those feelings now. Thank you so much Rudra.' My thoughts probed me as I boarded the flight.

DETACHMENT

Detachment is an important aspect of living a good life. Detachment is necessary because nothing in this world is permanent and we need to learn to detach from the things and people we love or the people who bring the negativity in our life.

When you lose something or someone dear to you or you go through a heart break or some other major loss, you feel the païn every moment. Going through such tough times, most of us try to suppress our tears, sorrow and grief thinking that it would make us better. But it is a wrong notion.

You can never get detached from an emotion which you try to suppress. You may feel a temporary relief for the moment, but it would become worse with time. We cannot control our emotions and when we try to do so, they express themselves in other forms. Just like a pressed spring jumps higher when released. If you try to curb your sadness, it may express itself as anger or irritation later on. So, let your emotions flow because that is what they are meant to be.

To get detached, we need to live those emotions to the fullest. Love with all your heart, express what you want to express, weep to your heart's content, be sad when you feel sad. You can only get detached from the people and things when you do not stop yourself from experiencing the pain.

Do not try to control things and let them happen as they have to. Detachment becomes easy when you accept yourself and your feelings as real, when you stop denying your feelings. When you stop lying to yourself that you are not sad and everything is perfectly fine.

Emotions are like a flowing river. When you try to stop them, you try to stop the flow of the river and this will only lead to flood i.e. mental stress, emotional trauma. You can never detach yourself in such conditions. While if you let the river flow, it may have flood during rainy days, but eventually everything would be normal with time, calm and peaceful.

Detachment is accepting life as it comes, learning to live without trying to hold on to anything or trying to feel what actually we do not feel. Detachment is the ultimate form of liberty which comes with acceptance. Accepting the God's wish, knowing that whatever happens has been planned and stores something good for us in the coming future. Accepting that nothing is permanent in this world. We all are here on this stage called earth to play our respective role and that everyone leaves when their part in the play is finished.

Acceptance is the key to detachment which gives you the ultimate peace and relieve from the emotional roller coasters we go through at different points of our lives.

CHAPTER 26

Aditya usually had a very busy schedule. There were many occasions when I felt like talking to him and share some important news but he was not there. Many times, I had to wait for hours for him to reply my calls and messages. It used to bother me and make me sad because when I wanted him to be with me to share my happiness or sorrow, he couldn't because of his schedule. I understood his work and the efforts he was putting in, but some important moments too never come back. I did not want to be the reason of distraction in his work as well. I knew that his work was his priority. So, it was difficult for me to be vocal about my need of talking to him sometimes.

I attended the award function in New Delhi. I wanted to meet Aditya, but he said he would be in New York for work. I understood, but my feelings and need made me feel apprehensive sometimes. I was upset that I wouldn't get to spend time with Aditya like I thought we would.

"Hi. How are you?" Came Aditya's much awaited voice from the phone.

"Hi, Aditya. I am good. I am still in Delhi, but I'll be leaving soon."

"I will be coming back to Delhi in two days. I too wanted to meet you, but you know I could not miss this meeting too. So, I had to come here. Where are you at present?"

I gave him the details of my hotel.

"I understand, Aditya."

I actually understood Aditya very well, but his careless attitude towards our relationship made me think otherwise. Sometimes, I felt may be I was expecting too much from a person so broke inside and some other time I felt Aditya needs my help. I felt clinging to him and wanted him to need me.

"Aditya was never as emotional as I am. He was very practical. Every person evolves in life. Every person changes because of his life. Aditya has seen a lot of hardships already and has evolved in the person; he is today. His work and his focus on work help him. He gives less priority to emotions and relationships because he deflects them. I should accept him as he is and let his role in my life unfold itself with time." I kept on talking to myself. It helped me get things in perspective. "Rudra was very different from Aditya. I loved him too at that time, but today its Aditya I am attached to. He is a totally different person. Our connection is different. It feels like a soul-connection. My heart knows it wouldn't be happy with Aditya, the way he is now, but all I need to understand is that my happiness resides within me. I need to stop depending on others for my happiness. No one is perfect. Am I? No. Then how can I ask him to be. I should not be bothered by Aditya's busy schedules and his inability to balance relationships and work. He has all the right to live his life as he wants. I need to wait and watch what life has in store for me." My reverie pacified me. I thought I felt relieved.

The loud ring of the phone in the hotel room brought me back from my thoughts. I wasn't expecting calls. Not from inside the hotel.

"Mam, you have a visitor in the hotel lobby." The formal tone of hotel staff came from the receiver.

"Visitor?" I wasn't expecting any visitor either, so this surprised me. "Who, did he say, he is?"

"Ma'am, he hasn't given his name. He is waiting in the

lobby. Should I tell him you are not available?"

"No. Wait. I'll be there in a minute."

I had no idea who it could be at this late hours, it was already ten.

Downstairs in lobby, I saw the back of a man in what looked like an Armani suit. His silhouette looked familiar, but to me all suit carrying men looked the same.

"Excuse me?"

"Did you like the surprise?" said Aditya while turning to face me. "Hi."

"Aditya.." suddenly my heart felt light to me. His easy smile on lips radiated to my heart. This surprise had made me happy. Really happy. "Oh my God! I loved the surprise."

"I came directly from airport. I just reached India and thought to surprise you. I couldn't let you leave without meeting me, now could I?"

I was so happy. I felt guilty for accusing him of not being emotional enough. This was indeed a huge surprise for me. Probably the best that he ever gave.

"Congrats, Aarohi. This was such a big day for you and I couldn't be there. I am so sorry. I feel so proud of you. Let me take you somewhere."

"I'll go get ready." I couldn't keep excitement out of my voice.

"Please... You are looking so pretty already. Let's not waste time. I want to spend all the time with you that I can."

I blushed. I couldn't believe it was him saying all this. He took my hand and we both proceeded towards his car.

Aditya drove around a little and parked the car near India Gate. The place looked lovely at night. 'More with him' I thought and smiled.

"Let's sit here for some time." He smiled too.

The night was peaceful. We both stood in front of India Gate which was emitting its aura and adding to the beauty of the night.

Aditya held my hand. He avoided looking in my eyes and kept looking at the lights.

"I know, Aarohi, that I fail to express my emotions many times when I should. By many times I mean almost all the times." He smiled sheepishly and looked into my eyes. "I know it hurts you and you feel ignored. You need to trust me because you have a very special place in my heart. You fill the void in my life which no one else in the world can, but at the same time, I do not know about my life. It's stagnant for the time being. I do not want to get married again. I am not mentally prepared for it right now. Right now, I like my life as it is, you, my work, my friends. I may want to get married in future, but I cannot assure that either. So, I do not want you to wait for me. I want you to move on in life, a bright future awaits you."

I looked into Aditya's eyes. His eyes, raw with the emotions that he must be feeling.

"You are not holding my hand for the first time Aditya. Your touch makes me feel that you have been holding my hand since ages. That I know that touch from some other life of mine. Maybe you are not able to feel that right now, but I can and I will wait for you to realize it. You don't have to worry about me because I am not waiting for you Aditya, I am waiting for my soulmate and my soul connects with you. You can take your time to recognize me."

Aditya looked into my eyes. Suddenly, his hands snaked around my shoulders and he hugged me. He hugged me tight, like he never had before. I got locked in his arms. Withdrawing from the hug, slowly he looked into my eyes with feelings trapped in two eyes of his. Before I could say anything, his lips met mine in a deep and passionate kiss. Suddenly, everything happening outside was no more in the picture for me. I was where I wanted to be. My insecurities, disappointment and sadness gave in. I could feel the solace I was looking for. The touch had sensitized me. I felt I was not embraced in these strong arms for the first time. I had been doing it since ages; may be in all my previous lives. A sense of belonging travelled through my body like a wave or current bringing all my nerves on fire.

I felt like I was the luckiest person on earth. I realized that I had found my soulmate. I could not lose him. I had found the place in his arms where my soul was at peace. We remained locked in the hug oblivious to the world around us. Nothing mattered to us, but each other.

SOULMATE

Our souls recognize their counterparts. They have their own sensors to receive signals if we allow them to. Many a times in life we come across people with whom we feel the instant connect and we wonder as to why the person seems so acquainted. Among our family and friends too there are some people whom we love and care from the depth of our heart. Our souls recognize them and our connections with them from our last births.

Being loved by someone is a wonderful feeling, but being understood is a feeling beyond words. You feel it every minute with your soulmate. You are lucky if you find such a person because not everyone finds this kind of love bond in life.

We can meet one or more soulmates in our lifetime and once you meet your soulmate, it's almost impossible to ignore them. You may stay away from them, but your heart will never get detached because they are a part of your soul. We just need to listen to the voice of our soul because our soul keeps looking for its soulmates and the kind of love it deserves. You feel relieved and happy once you are with your soulmate.

CHAPTER 27

Finally, the day came. I had to submit my thesis today. The day started with the completion of formalities required before submission of thesis. It was a procedure requiring certain signatures and other formalities which consumed most of the time of the day. As oppose to the glamorous portrays of movies and TV shows, it mostly is a hectic schedule of paperwork. Finally, when I was done, I headed towards the Administrative Building. Paying all the pending dues, I waited for another half an hour when I was provided with the clearance and I proceeded towards the Thesis Section.

I looked at my thesis another moment, with pride and a feeling of mixed emotions clouded my vision. Then I submitted the thesis. Walking out of the Thesis section, standing on the stairs, I saw the elevated view of the university and thought 'Is that it? My Ph.D. is over? What do I do next?'

I had to appear for the Ph.D. Viva after six months' which was the last formality left in my Ph.D. completion. I needed to figure out my path, my next step. I was relieved as well as anxious.

I called up mom.

"It's over mom." A relief and fear was evident in my pride mixed voice.

"Congratulations, Aarohi. Now, you must be free to enjoy your day and your life too." Mom hinted about Aditya, about whom I told her in my last visit. Though mom did not say anything about Aditya's age or divorcee status, her response was not very encouraging as well, but I knew, she wasn't a mother who would say no just because I told her about it. She was a mother who would think well before letting me on. Today, she sounded more playful and hopeful.

"Aarohi, you were always an old soul, my darling. I always knew that. You were more grown up for your age, more matured. I can understand that you could be happy with only that person who is more matured and sorted than you are. I have been thinking about it since the day you told me about Aditya. I think I feel confident about your choice as I know you so well and I too understand that it is the qualities in a person that really matter. Everything else is secondary. If my daughter is confident about the love of her life, I will always be there by her side. I am happy that you found one like yourself." She started laughing on phone. "I told your dad and convinced him too. Now when are we going to meet him?"

"Soon, mom."

I was very excited to go home. I had had my share of home sickness in past few days. I wanted to hug my family and talk to them and eat Gobhi-ke-paranthe made by mom.

I also sent an email a few days back to Aakriti about Aditya with his picture as she was very much curious to see him. Aakriti had all the right in the world to know about him. She was the reason I could find love and meet my soulmate in life.

While packing my stuff to back home I got an email from Aakriti. A big 'CONGRATULATIONS' in the subject line and a small message.

Aarohi, you were always the most special person I ever knew. Be the same always. You will reach the sky and touch those heights you never knew you could, but I always knew.

Hey. Aditya looks great. I saw the picture.

I love you, sista. You are the best.

Love,

Aakriti

PS: I want to meet Aditya.

I grinned reading her email. Aakriti had all the flamboyance of becoming a writer. That's what she wanted to do in life. I knew how much Aakriti would have wanted to know more details about Aditya. 'You gotta wait for me to come back, sista.' I smiled to myself on the thought.

I decided to spend some time with her after past stressed and hurried days. I wanted to have my share of mother's love and sister's leg pulling. I realized I was out for so long. Next month I had to leave for China for a conference and that will start my new journey in life. I boarded a sleeper bus and left for home at night.

I was trying to sleep in the bus, but it was difficult as the bus was on a bumpy ride and the driver was having his fun pretending the bus was a roller coaster. Suddenly, my phone which was lying beside me beeped and lit up. There was a message and it was from Aditya.

What if I did not realize that you are my soulmate? Would you leave me?

I smiled to myself. I could guess the leg pulling Aditya was attempting.

Then I will marry Rahul.

Phone beeped again.

Rahul?

Single word followed with an eye raised smiley.

Yeah. He is my dad's friend's son. He came back from America and will meet me home.

I smiled on my teasing him. Next message came sooner than I expected.

I am coming to your house too. Wanted to meet your parents anyway.

I double read to ensure what it meant. It didn't change. I felt excitement rising in me. Was that true?

Are you serious?

Next reply came in a little late. 'Or was it just me thinking?'

Yes, I want to meet you and your family too. Only if you are comfortable that is.

I'd love that, but are you sure?

Yes, Aarohi. I am. As sure as I am of you.

A heart emoticon this time. My excitement grew and I started smiling like a school kid.

I would reach home by tomorrow morning and would love to introduce you to them. Tell me whenever you can reach there and I'll tell my parents about it.

Hmm... Done.

Still out with your colleagues?

Yes. I miss you...

The message gave a jolt to my already happy and racing heart. I felt happier and I never thought that it was even possible. I submitted my thesis, got a nod for my relationship with Aditya from mom and was also going home- all in a day. And then this. I happily typed my response.

Me too...

Will give you a call tomorrow. Have a safe journey. I love you.

I love you too.

Aditya's messages kept me wondering about the future of our relationship. *When I had opened the tight fists of my mind and had let go of every expectation, everything was coming to me as destined.* I wanted to follow the same path and did not want to try to control my life. Thinking about Aditya and the present time in my life, my mind happily revolved in thoughts and drifted off to sleep.

I had to leave everything and go. I did not understand where I was going and was feeling helpless. I was trying to call mom, dad and Aakriti . I was looking at Aditya, helpless, as if asking him to accompany me, but he was unable to do that. No one was listening to me. I was shouting and calling them at top of my voice, but no one was listening. Then I finally realized that I was actually alone, was always alone, came into this world alone and have to leave this world alone. The sudden realization hit me badly and I started to pant...

I woke up from the dream, but this time I was feeling very peaceful. I was mostly panicked from such dreams, but now I had no such feelings. I realized that I had reached my hometown. I got down hurriedly from the bus, collected my luggage and boarded an auto rickshaw to reach my home. My heart was awaiting the hugs of my family.

DISCOVER YOURSELF

Life is magical. It's just that we are afraid to accept it. Not everyone has the guts to discover life and oneself. You need to explore your soul layer by layer to find the person that you are. Spending and sparing time to listen to your heart is what everyone needs to do. The depth of soul cannot be measured, you need to keep digging. While we are busy with the worldly tasks, our home, job, interaction with others, socializing, we tend to feel that this is what life is. Most of the people spend their life doing this work and home cycle and die with the regret of not living their life.

Everyone is a role model for someone. A boss may be a role model for his subordinates, a mother for her children and a leader for his followers. You can inspire those around you and help them find their path in life which in itself is a great service to the mankind.

A time may come in your life, when you actually want to understand the purpose of your life and existence. Then these worldly things become secondary; and the person who is always with you- you become important for yourself. You are keen to know the depth of your soul, your feelings and your existence. You start understanding reasons for meeting certain people, the reasons for your emotional attachments as well as detachments.

You may want to understand that why do people around you change with time. Change is the part of life, but some things which should not change with time are being in touch with yourself, keeping the child in you alive, the innocence and the qualities in you. We need to discover ourselves whenever we feel lost or too much involved and impacted by the outside world.

The basic nature of all living beings is the same. Just like plants, you too become dead inside when detached from the roots. It is important to be in touch with our roots, the person that we are, listening to ourselves, doing things which soothe our soul, following our dreams and do everything to nourish our roots.

CHAPTER 28

I was sitting at the rock hill top; the one I had visited with Aakriti, the last time. This time I went there alone. I loved to celebrate my happy and special moments in life by spending time at peace with nature. Everything there was same, the river, the sky, mountains, trees...everything. Only I was different, I had grown personally and become a person who was trying to improve every day.

I was holding the job offer letter from the Best Research Centre in India which had arrived at my home just before me. Suddenly, the vibration in the mobile phone caught my attention. I was hoping it would be Aditya's call as he was coming to meet me and was on his way. I was happy to see my wish coming true. Aditya was calling me.

"Where are you?"

"You are driving?"

"Yes. Your turn."

"I am at that hill I told you about."

"Okay. Will take around three more hours for me."

"I am waiting."

"Bye. I love you."

"I love you too." I smiled, 'that will take time to get used to' I thought. Aditya kept giving me surprises since that chat in bus. Now, I was eagerly waiting for him to arrive and wanted to share the news about my job personally. I was sure he would be happy since I would be placed in Delhi too. I was sure we will get more time together now.

Looking at the beautiful view, I was thinking about my life. I thought about my love for Aditya. It was the love without expectations, selfless and unconditional, love of the soulmates where we understood each other so well that there was no space left for other expectations. I had understood that loving someone does not always mean you have to be with them.

Sometimes, you meet someone in your life at a point when you are in great need to understand your self-worth. You need to understand that you are still capable of being loved, of being of utmost importance to someone. It does not mean that you need to lose the other important things and relationships. Everyone comes in our life for a purpose, to teach us something or simply to remind us of our own importance.

However, if you are destined to be together, you would be and vice versa. Trying to control things and expecting everything as you planned is not the best thing to do. We need to accept everything in life as it comes.

There are relationships which are very close to our heart and the feelings which cannot fade in intensity with time. Sometimes, even the time gap or not being in touch does not fade the intensity of love. Classifying relationships is a complex job. It's better to feel every relationship as crude as it comes and not try to understand the logics behind our feelings.

I had started to expect less from myself, had stopped blaming myself for the failures and was finding more peace within myself. Earlier I used to be worried about the future and tried to find answers to the questions about the events in my life, but with time I had understood to take life as it comes and live in the present moment without trying to find answers to the questions life stores in for us. As much as I understood it I fell in love with my life.

Going down the memory lane, I thought about Rudra. How I felt after the heart-break and how I feel about it now? I thought about ups and downs in my Ph.D. journey, about the people I met who knowingly as well as unknowingly helped me to grow in life as well as professionally.

I had realized with time that the kind of people, relationships and situations we attract in our life depends on us. Everything happens for reason. The reason however, may not be clear now, but definitely unfolds with time. With these thoughts running through my mind, I was enjoying the pleasant weather and scenic beauty.

I closed my eyes and felt the serenity of the moment. Happily, I thanked God for this beautiful life and this lovely moment. I was having my family by my side, a man who loved me and a job I always dreamt to do. I loved it all, but yet I was detached from everything. I knew that in the end I am alone and my happiness should not depend on anything other than myself. I was happy with the freedom I was feeling within me and the courage I had gathered over time to explore myself.

I was happily walking on path of Self Awakening and Exploration and everything was falling in place automatically. I was grateful to God for helping me realize that the happiness I was trying to find everywhere and in others was actually to be searched within me.

I opened my eyes, put on my favorite music on the mobile phone and plugged in the earphones. Smiling, I checked my watch. I had spent past twenty minutes thinking about things that happened in my life, but now I had to go home and cook a surprise for Aditya. I wanted to surprise him.

I got up and brushed my jeans. One look at the setting sun and I turned to leave.

"Whoa! Aditya?"

"Hi. Surprise."

"Oh my God! You have developed a habit, mister."

"I hope you like it."

"I am not sure." I teased him and his eyes smiled with his lips. "Depends on what else I get."

Aditya looked in my eyes; smile vanishing from his lips and a soft expression taking its place.

"What?" I looked in his eyes.

"This is what you get." He pulled out a velvet covered box out of his blue jeans pocket, my favorite jeans, and pulled the small lid in front of me. There rested a beautiful small ring with one diamond in middle. Beautiful and simple; just like our relationship.

Every nerve ending in my body was firing heavily and my heart filled with overwhelming happiness as I looked in his eyes. Tears threatened to flow down, but I controlled myself. I wouldn't want to blur this vision with tears. I wanted to remember this for life.

"Aren't you supposed to go down on your knee?"

"I can do that."

"You don't have to."

Aditya laughed heartily.

"Ready?" I nodded.

"Aarohi, you are an amazing, amazing women. I am rusty on details of what I read, but I know we can make an amazing life together. I have grown with you in such a small time. Grown out of bitterness; grown in love. You make me happy and I love to do that for you. I love surprising you and seeing your reactions and want to keep doing that all life; all lives even. Marry me."

Tears started glistening in my eyes as I nodded and Aditya wore me the ring. Aditya's hand slipped down my back and he pulled me into a hug, whispering "Thank you" in my ear. I kept hugging him back as I looked into the setting sun. A promise of a new morning and a beautiful starry night in the air.

Why do we fear the night? Why do we not give our hardships equal love? They are the ones that make us. They are the ones that pave path for beautiful glory of sun in morning.

I held Aditya's hand against setting sun while we started moving down the hill. I had a promise of beautiful life ahead.

Also by Rooprashi

The Ascent Of Love

Take a peek into the adventurous life of a mountaineer through this motivational and emotional love story.

When Taara met Vedant, she fell in love for the first time. However, she could not perceive that a feeling as pure as love can turn into something so toxic for her.

As she decided to leave her love behind and climb peaks of the world, she knew that the love for the peaks was not hers either.

As she questions herself and is inept to understand why she is not able to forget her past, her ascent to the peaks was making the difference apparent to her. Something she already knew.

Had she found a new love, or was love back in an old package to spite her again? Does a difficult mountaineering course in Kashmir prove to be the turning point in her life? Will she be able to complete her 'Ascent of Love' the way she intended to, or will a storm change plan of her life?

"The Ascent Of Love is a story encrypted with motivation and intellect that is highly gripping yet heart-touching. It is recommended to everyone to have a positive outlook in life."

- Radhakrishnan Pillai, Author of 8 Bestsellers